Qualified as a vet from Cambridge university, Alastair's first job was with RSPCA in Putney. He spent five years as a vet in Southern Africa before briefly coming back to the UK, then went out to Bahrain as a horse vet to Shaikh Isa. During the First Gulf War, Alastair decided to come back to the UK and set up a practice with his wife, Caryn. He took early retirement in 2016 and now they enjoy living with their pets in the Béarn in France.

To Charlotte, Katheryn and James

Alastair England

THE VETILANTE

Memoirs of a
Veterinary Psychopath

AUSTIN MACAULEY PUBLISHERS™
LONDON • CAMBRIDGE • NEW YORK • SHARJAH

A CIP catalogue record for this title is available from the British Library.

ISBN 9781035821518 (Paperback)
ISBN 9781035821525 (Hardback)
ISBN 9781035821549 (ePub e-book)
ISBN 9781035821532 (Audiobook)

www.austinmacauley.co.uk

First Published 2024
Austin Macauley Publishers Ltd®
1 Canada Square
Canary Wharf
London
E14 5AA

I would like to thank the staff and patients of all the charities I have worked with; The RSPCA in Putney, the Animal Welfare in Cape Town and the RSPCA South East Essex branch, especially Bonnie and Marilyn. I have to thank all the staff and animals I have worked with at Earls Hall in Southend for their patience. I would also like to thank Austin Macauley for publishing this book.

Table of Contents

The shrouded body slid effortlessly into the sea that greedily sucked it in with a satisfying slurp. It was like hearing the "clink" when putting an empty wine bottle into the bottle bank and it hits the broken glass. I suppose this was recycling of a sort.

The sea was calm and the moon light shimmied on the inky water. I loved being out on the water at night. It was soothing and relaxing.

I checked the chart plotter. With this incoming tide, it should take just over an hour to motor back to the marina; I should be at there at high tide. I liked off-loading the bodies before high tide so that went I got back to the marina, it was high tide and easier to dock the boat as the berths were narrow and at right angles to the tide. I had found a deeper area just past the Whittaker buoy on the Maplin Sands to dump them. I thought that when the tide went out, it helped bury them in the sand. This would be the second in two days.

I had killed more people, but lately had taken to disposing of them at sea. With each one, I became more proficient. I am not sure what I should call them; bodies, corpses or the remains of human scum who had abused animals and caused unnecessary suffering. There was a gentle westerly wind but it was too dark to put up the sails. The boat lights were on: time for a cup of tea.

I went downstairs into the cabin, lit the gas stove and put on the kettle. There was a large black and white cat asleep on the bed. I stroked his head and he purred without opening his eyes, nudging my hand affectionately. I should go back up on deck but there wasn't much to bump into out here apart from the odd fishing boat and any debris floating in the Crouch.

I put some food into the empty cat bowl and went upstairs to tidy the deck. It amazed me how unobservant people were. I wheeled the bodies from the car park, along the pontoon to the boat in a trolley. A few carefully placed empty cardboard boxes and a blanket hid my cargo from view. Even those living on the house boats would wave and carry on. I had adapted the anchor winch to help me pull them onto the boat. Once onboard, I twisted four meters of anchor chain around them secured it with a padlock then wrapped it all in an old piece of sail which I stitched whilst I was going out to sea. It just looked like I was mending something.

I had bought the boat second-hand. The previous owner had worked hard and saved up to enjoy sailing it. But his wife put an end to his dreams. It was either her or the boat. He was someone who planned for every eventuality as it had come with a spare set of sails—gib, mainsail and spinnaker.

It also had a very long length of anchor chain which was proving very useful.

I had a motor home I called Possy which I modified to have a large fridge under the bed. It had been originally used to store wine. I bought the bodies to the marina in this. I had slept in the mobile home once with a body in the fridge but I had had terrible nightmares that the victim was trying to get out.

I went downstairs to make a mug of tea, grabbed a biscuit from the tin above the cooker and went back on deck. There was bit of time before I would get back to the marina.

The Couch narrowed here and I could hear the clinking rigging of moored boats as the masts swayed in the wash.

Maybe I had better explain why I was recycling people in the River Crouch.

Anti-Mortem

Let me start at the beginning.

My parents were at school with each other. My father was a mediocre student who longed to excel at sport but never did. I think that he thought if he hung around the best sportsman, some of their talent would rub off on him. It didn't. But he had a good memory and became a very good bridge and poker player. He taught me to play the former and played the latter very successfully to supplement his income.

He left school at eighteen and got a job in an accounting firm as a clerk which he still has today.

My mother was the only child with wealthy parents and from the age of seventeen developed passions for horses and sex.

On her nineteenth birthday, she got pregnant; by whom she never said, but she managed to persuade my father to marry her: with the financial help of her parents.

She needn't have bothered as she lost the baby, but for whatever reason, she was happy to get married to my father. It suited my father for although he had no interest in sex, he certainly did enjoy the generosity of his in-laws.

Every evening my father would have two cans of IPA which he would meticulously pour into a pint mug he was given for his eighteenth birthday and slowly sip whilst watching television. By the end of the evening, it was warm and flat, but he didn't seem to mind. One New Year's Eve, my mother laced his beer with several shots of vodka and then seduced him on the settee. Nine months later, my sister was born at the end of August. She did the same thing five years later and nine months later, I was born at the beginning of September. My sister and my birthdays were 10 days apart. As hers was before mine, I always seemed to get short-changed with presents. But Nana made it up with cash she secretly gave me.

It was my sister who told me about my mother spiking my father's drink during one of the few conversations we had together. Whether it was true or not I didn't know but the idea of doctoring someone's drink stuck with me. Why my mother had children I don't know; she never showed any real interest in us or any love.

Early years at school were awful for me. I was constantly bullied and picked on by the local kids who knew my mother's reputation, which was amplified at the school gate.

In desperation, my grandparents paid for me to go to a prep school boarding as a weekly boarder. It was far enough away that I was unknown. At first, it was difficult as I was an outsider but I learnt how to avoid trouble; how not to be seen.

I wasn't different enough or interesting enough for the older boys so they left me alone and picked some other unfortunates. I kept myself to myself. But I did enjoy some of the school activities such as martial arts and shooting. The school had a small range with rifles and pistols. I would line up on the target and imagine I was shooting someone I didn't like. The martial arts gave me strength in body and in mind.

I failed the common entrance because I had no desire to go to public school and so was sent to the local comprehensive. As I was early September-born, I was the eldest in the class. Those who had bullied me at primary school could see that during the years I had spent at prep school, I had grown taller and muscled so they avoided me. There were other softer targets. For those who had bullied me before, I realised how to get revenge. Tamper with sports kit, remove studs or tie-up laces. I would rip out vital pages of homework. It was anonymous and petty but I got pleasure from it and it was untraceable as there was no CCTV. I enjoyed seeing hassled boys late for sports or being marked down for homework. Definite schadenfreude.

I didn't have any real friends and my mother was busy playing horses and my father playing cards so I spent weekend afternoons roaming the fields behind our house where there were some ponies. One of them was a lively chestnut gelding with four white socks and a blaze on his nose. He had a smart leather head collar with "Buster" engraved on a shiny tag. The school caterer's favourite vegetable was carrots which they cooked in long strips, "Al dente". I would take an extra portion which I wrapped up in a tissue and put in my pocket to feed the ponies. I would walk up to them and stoke them. Buster would sniff round my pockets desperate for the carrots. He grew to trust me. I would tickle his muzzle and scratch behind his ears. He used to follow me round the field hoping for more carrots and he would even canter over to me when I called his name.

One day he was gone. I felt a little lost and empty. I had always looked forward to seeing him and giving him a stroke.

A few days later, my mother took me to the yard where she kept her horse. I was off school with a cold and for some reason, she didn't want to leave me at home on my own.

She had been having an affair with the local vet since she had married my father and he was at the yard treating her horse.

Suddenly, there was a loud metallic bang and several yells and Buster came flying round the corner chased by an overweight woman in tight fitting purple jodhpurs.

Without thinking, I grabbed the lead rein. Buster's eyes were full of panic but the fear melted away as I talked to him.

'Steady Buster. Steady.'

He started nuzzling my head and then sniffed my pockets for carrots.

'Sorry boy. I haven't got any.' I laughed and scratched his nose. He nodded playfully.

'That's incredible.' The vet was smiling at me. 'Your son has a real way with animals, Alice. There could have been a nasty accident.' He turned towards the yard gate which opened onto a busy road.

The woman in the purple jodhpurs took Buster from me.

'What happened?' The vet asked.

'Some scaffolding poles fell over spooking the new livery. Some idiot hadn't tied him up properly.' My mother scowled at the woman in the purple jodhpurs. The woman blushed the colour of her jodhpurs and nervously led Buster away.

The vet turned towards me. 'You've obviously got a way with animals. Would you like a job? We'll pay you. We need someone to help with the animals on Saturday afternoons.'

I nodded and spluttered my thanks before my mother could say anything. The following Saturday I did my homework in the morning had a quick lunch and got to the vets at 2 o'clock.

Thripe, Eager and Thomas MRCVS's was a well-established veterinary practice in an old Edwardian building near the centre of town. It was about 10 minutes' walk away from our house. The three partners had all retired but the practice decided to keep the name as everyone knew it.

I was given a pale blue scrub top and led to the back if the practice where I discovered my job was cleaning out soiled stainless steel cages. I loved it.

As the staff got to trust me, I was allowed to do more and I learnt to handle dogs, cats and various small furies. I especially liked hamsters. I was taught how to hold the animals for injections by the nurses and found that the animals seemed to trust me. I knew that I wanted to be a vet.

My sister had left school at 18 with very little to show for apart from an addiction to cigarettes and soft drugs. As she was August-born, she was the youngest in her class.

When I was born, she was filled with jealousy. She wanted the attention my mother had had as an only child. My earliest memories were of her pinching me in the car on the way to a family holiday in Cornwall. We never got on; at best there was indifference between us, at worst a deep festering hate.

When I got the Saturday job at the vet's, my mother persuaded the main hairdressers in town "Jerome and Paul" to take my sister on as an apprentice. They were happy to do so as they were always losing trainees to other salons. Jerome and Paul was gossip central as all of the school mothers who were anybody went there every 6 weeks to have their roots re dyed, their fringes trimmed and find out who was sleeping, or not sleeping, with whom. My mother had given up going there as she was often the centre of the rumour mill, probably unfairly, but my sister was happy to supply her with all the gory details.

As my sister had left school and had a full-time job, my parents decided she should pay board and lodging. Although she shouted and screamed at my father, he was uncharacteristically firm and in the end, my sister gave in. She was paid weekly in cash on a Friday and before she was allowed to go out, she paid a third of her wages to my mother. This meant that after going out Friday and Saturday nights, she was inevitably broke. She would plead poverty and my mother would hand over money for information.

When I started work at the vet's, my sister demanded that I pay rent but when my father pointed out that I was still at school and when she was my age she refused to get a job; she had no counter argument.

She worked Tuesday to Saturday finishing at 5.00pm when she would come home tired and hungry. The hairdresser had a small back room where the staff could take a break and a back yard where they could smoke a cigarette. When she got home, she would raid the fridge for anything sweet and go upstairs to the bathroom where she would spend an hour getting herself ready to go into town at about 7.00pm. I finished work then so I knew that if I walked home slowly she would be gone by the time I came back and I wouldn't have to see her until she emerged late Sunday morning.

It suited both of us and for a while we had an uneasy truce. But as I earned money, I was able to buy CDs and books. I even brought myself a small stereo system I had in my room.

After a while, I noticed books and CDs going missing. I knew it was my sister but couldn't prove it so I bought a padlock so I could lock them in my wardrobe.

But one Monday I came back from school and found the wardrobe broken and my CDs scratched and my books scribbled on and pages torn out.

I was furious and rushed downstairs to complain to my parents but my mother just shrugged her shoulders. She didn't want to upset her spy in the hairdressers and my father had the look of someone not wanting another of my sister's tirades, or going against his wife.

My sister laughed and claimed that it was a poltergeist. After that, possessions meant little to me and I opened a building society account and invested my wages in that.

One Saturday a client brought in a hamster in a big plastic cage and a bag of food. His daughter was allergic to it and they had to find a new home. I would do anything to re-home it. To have my own pet. That would be amazing. The duty nurse saw the look of desperation on my face.

'All right. If your parents agree, then you can take it home.'

I couldn't believe it. I grabbed my coat and hurried home. My father was watching sport on the television.

'Can I have a hamster, Dad?'

My father rubbed his chin. I could see all he wanted to watch the football.

'I can keep it in my room. No-one will know that it is in the house.'

My father didn't look away from the TV but nodded his agreement.

I rushed out of the house and back to the practice.

'My father says I can take it home with me. Is it a boy or girl?' I asked.

'It's a boy called Hammy,' the nurse replied, laughing.

I took Hammy home with me. My sister was out and my mother was with her horse.

My father looked up when I started to go upstairs.

'Make sure it stays in your room and doesn't cause any problems.'

I nodded and took Hammy upstairs.

It was several days before my mother found out. She was a bit put out at first. But when she saw how clean and quiet he was, she agreed that I could keep him.

My sister was furious.

'Why can he have a pet? Anyway, it's a rat. It's vermin.' She refused to be in the same room as me and claimed the noise of the hamster going round in its wheel at night kept her awake. But gradually, things went back to normal.

I didn't really care. Hammy was gentle and happy for me to handle him. He was very clean using the same part of his cage for his toilet. I would watch him eat stuffing nuts into his cheek pouches. I made him a maze out of the cardboard inner tubes of kitchen roll which he enjoyed going through. At night time, the whirring of his wheel was somehow comforting and it always sent me to sleep.

The staff at the vets treated me as one on their own. Whenever there was a staff birthday, cakes would be brought in and Wendy, the head receptionist, would make sure something was saved for me to have when I came in on

Saturday afternoon. I demolished them with relish. Clients were always bringing in things they no longer needed; drugs, food, blankets and newspapers that were used for bedding. One day someone had bought in a half full bag of hamster food they didn't want any more. Wendy asked if I wanted it for Hammy. She told me it was on a table in the prep room. It was an expensive brand and there were some seeds in a dish next to it so I tipped them into the bag which I took home when I finished work. I would give it to him when he finished the cheap brand I had bought him.

A few days later, when I came back from school the front door was open and so my mother and sister didn't hear me come in. They were talking loudly in the kitchen.

'Jerome says there are rats in the staffroom. He's called the council to put some poison down. He says there is a big problem in town especially in the council flats but he is too mean to pay for it himself.' My sister's laugh was hollow.

'I've been there for nearly a year and there's no sign of a pay rise. All I do is wash hair, help put on the dye and sweep up. Tracey Newton says Dean in Leigh is looking for staff. Maybe I should go there.' I came into the room and they both shut up.

I didn't think any more about it until that fateful day.

It was the following Monday. My father went to work as usual. I fed and watered Hammy. I started the new food and he seemed to like it. Then I went to school with double math followed by double science. I was due to get my homework back. Last week I had been top of the class and I was hoping for the same. Exams were coming up soon. My mother was making a token effort at housework and my sister was in her still in her room.

When I got back from school, I was tired and annoyed. Ellie Hastings had gotten higher marks than me. As I walked into my room I knew at once something wasn't right. It was silent. I rushed over to Hammy's cage but there was no movement. At first, I couldn't see him. Then I saw him lying flat out. He didn't seem to be breathing. I threw the top off the cage. He didn't move. When I picked him up, he felt still and cold. I suspected the worst. I looked in his feed bowl. There were some strange blue seeds in it. I heard a stifled laugh and I turned to see my sister staring at me in the doorway with a strange grin on her face. I grabbed Hammy with some of the seeds, pushed past my sister and ran out of the house to the vets.

I could see from their faces that Hammy was dead.

The vet looked at the seed than went out of the consulting room. She came back with a small book that had 'poisons' on the front.

'Where did you get this seed?' She asked.

'I found it in his cage. I don't know where it came from. I'm the only person who feeds him.'

The vet put her hand on my shoulder. 'Hammy's been poisoned. These seeds are laced with warfarin. They are designed to kill rats and mice. We've had a few clients bringing them in. I think the council have been using them.' My shoulders slumped and I took Hammy home to bury in the garden.

I cried for days and bought a small rose bush from the garden centre to put over him.

In the end, I couldn't stand the sight of his empty cage in my room. I asked the vets to give it to someone else. I don't know what happened but the next day, it was gone.

My father was reasonably sympathetic and mumbled that they didn't live very long any way. I suspect my mother was relieved it had gone and there was no danger of escaping and my sister just laughed at his death.

I just knew she had something to do with it. I just knew it. Then I remembered the conversation she had had with my mother that I had overheard.

She had done it deliberately. She had gotten the poison from work. That's why she was grinning at me in the doorway of my room.

My tears stopped then and I started to plan. I wanted to get revenge on my sister. I wanted the satisfaction of laughing at her misfortune.

My mother sometimes took a small dose of Valium at night. We knew when she had taken it because ten minutes after coming out of the bathroom, she would fall asleep in front of the television.

Clients were always bringing in unused boxes when their pets passed away. These were put in a box labelled RSPCA. The vets used these drugs for charity cases so the owners didn't have to pay. One of the senior vets in the practice liked prescribing diazepam for older dogs. I managed to get hold of a box of 10 milligram diazepam tablets that a client had returned. This was a much higher dose that my mother took. All I needed was the bait. I didn't have to wait long.

One of the trainee nurses bought in some chocolate brownies for her birthday and Wendy had saved me one. I cut it in two and ate one half. It was delicious full of nuts and dates. Perfect. I wrapped the half in silver foil and took it home when I had finished work and put it out of sight in the fridge.

That Saturday night my sister had been invited to charity ball at the local golf club. It was the biggest event in the town's social calendar. It was black tie and by invitation only. It gave the great and the good a chance to dress up in their finest. My sister's hairdressers was running flat out and my mother listened as my sister gave her the gossip. She had talked about nothing else for weeks. With a look of smug triumph, she announced she had persuaded John Carter to invite her. His father was the captain of the golf club and they lived in a huge mansion and drove the latest cars. All her friends were green with envy.

My mother was both proud and jealous; my father indifferent. When at school, he had tried golf but had failed to find most of the greens and been the laughing stock of his class mates. He had got his revenge by relieving them of the hard earned cash at the poker table. John Carter was one of his "victims". That week I planned what I would do. I would make sure she didn't go to the ball. I went through the timings over and over in my head. I broke the bathroom lock on Thursday evening. It was always breaking. If it did, it was a family rule to hang a towel on the door outside if you were using the bathroom. I muttered my apologies to my father who said he would fix it on Sunday morning; as I knew he would. That's when he always did any DIY.

On the Friday night, I took the brownie out of the fridge and waited for it to soften. Then I pushed three of the diazepam tablets into it, smoothing the sides of the brownie afterwards. When I inspected my handiwork, it was impossible to see where the tablets were. I wrapped it back in the foil and replaced it in the fridge.

My sister got ready to go to work as usual. I could see through her bedroom door her newly cleaned pink prom dress hanging on a hanger wrapped in cellophane. She scowled at me as she shut her bedroom door, complaining about the broken bathroom door then announced to no-one in particular she would be going to her prom with John Carter that evening. His parents were picking her up at 7.30. Not if I had anything to do with it! My mother was going down the yard to see her horse and was hoping to hack out that afternoon with 'the girls' and wouldn't be back until after eight o'clock.

I did my homework and ate a quick lunch. My father was installed in front of the television watching the cricket. I took the brownie out of the foil and placed it invitingly in the front of the fridge on a small plate on the second shelf just where my sister would see it. Then I went to work at the vets.

Saturday afternoons in the summer were busy at the vets. Animals were going home and new ones coming in as fast as I could clean the cages. I was worried I wouldn't be able to get home and see the fruits of my labour first hand. Evening surgery was from 4.00pm to 6.00pm and was fully booked so the duty vet and nurse were fully occupied. I put newspaper down in all the empty cages and topped up all the inpatients water.

I looked at my watch. It was 5.30pm. Five minutes to go. A nurse came through asking if I could hold a dog for a dressing change. The Jack Russell wouldn't stop wriggling and we had to change the dressing on a stitch-up on its tail. These were difficult even on well-behaved dogs. But eventually, we managed. The nurse said that wound looked OK and together we managed to restrain the dog long enough put on another.

The nurse took the dog through. It was 5.45pm. I was running late.

I went home as fast as I could; making sure no-one saw me. I crept into the house; my father was watching cricket on TV and I could hear the shower upstairs. I hurried up the stairs two at a time and pushed the bathroom door open.

My sister was lying in the bath. She had fallen and hit her head on the side of the bath.

There were bloodstains on the bath. Cinderella wouldn't be going to the ball tonight. John Carter would be really annoyed and my sister would be the laughing stock of her friends. I had had my revenge and seen her humiliation.

What I should have done is gone back to the vets happy I had avenged Hammy's death. How my life would have been different.

But as I looked at my sister lying helpless in the bath, all of the hate that had built up over the years engulfed me. I put on the disposable gloves I had taken from the vets. I turned the shower off, put the plug in the bath and ran the water as fast as I could into the bath. It filled up quickly. My sister groaned but her eyes stayed shut. When the water was high enough, I pushed my sister's head below the water. At first, she didn't struggle. When the water went into her lungs, she seemed to come alive. But she was weak and I easily held her under and soon she stopped struggling and went limp.

I turned the bath water off and turned the shower back on. As an afterthought, I took three tablets of my mother's Valium and put them in my pocket before hurrying downstairs back to the vets. I went straight to the staff toilet; closed the door and flushed my mother's tablets down it. When I came out, I went back into the kennels noisily and started work. No-one had noticed my absence. A warm sense of elation ran through my body. It was like nothing I had ever felt before. It was a feeling of power and I wanted to feel it again. It was addictive.

I tried to be as visual as possible helping and hindering the staff. I left work late and ambled home. When I turned the corner, there was an ambulance, a police car and a large silver Mercedes. The policeman and a paramedic were talking to the Carters who were dressed in their evening wear. I recognised them as clients of the veterinary practice. Their son was sitting in the car sniffling into a tissue.

My father was in the doorway, pale and drawn. There was no sign of my mother.

'Looks like a terrible accident,' the policeman said to no-one in particular.

My father looked at me with tears in his eyes and told me to go to my room. I could see my mother in the lounge with a large wine glass.

I went into my bedroom and closed the door. I felt elated. There was no guilt, no remorse.

No-one doubted that it was a tragic accident. She had slipped in the bath, knocked her head and drowned. She had probably taken the tablets to calm her nerves before the ball. Hammy had been avenged.

If I had thought my parents would have more time for me, I was mistaken. After the funeral, they barely talked to each other, let alone me. I had cried for ages when Hammy died but I didn't shed one tear for my sister. In fact, I think Hammy's death was the last time I cried.

My sister's belongings were packed up and taken to a charity shop and my father moved into her room.

I had no idea if my sister had a post-mortem and or if the diazepam was found but my mother started drinking even more heavily. She seemed to have an air of guilt about her and the Valium disappeared from the bath room. When "The Chase" came on TV in the evening, the first cork was popped. Later she progressed onto wine boxes.

My father joined a serious poker school in the East End of London and was often out all night playing, and wining.

It was only years later when I was writing it down that I remembered tipping the seeds into the opened hamster food bag Wendy had put aside for me. Those seeds had been brought in by someone else thinking a neighbour was trying to poison their dog, and they had been blue.

Wendy later confessed that she had put them there for the vet to look at and had forgotten all about it. I had killed Hammy.

But by this time, I was so far down my path it was too late for regrets.

M.R.C.V.S.

My GCSEs and "A" levels were good enough to be offered a place at the RVC: The Royal Veterinary College. After my sister's death, I worked as much as I could at the vets and started working more shifts during the summer holidays. The money and the experience were welcome.

Working at the vets also gave me an introduction to the concept of euthanasia. The public often bought in ill or injured wildlife; the majority of which were too sick or injured to treat. The nurses would relieve the public of their charge with a sympathetic smile; take the poor creature into the prep room and painlessly administer the dark blue liquid by injection. This lethal injection was pentobarbitone. There were also stray animals that had been run over or attacked or just old, and if they weren't been microchipped, so the owners could be traced, they would be given pain relief until the fatal decision was made.

The public would also bring in their pets which were nearing the end of their life. I would stand at the back of the consulting room listening to the vets sympathetically setting out the options. The clients would inevitably ask the vets 'what would you do?' The younger vets would often be reluctant to advise "putting to sleep", but the more experienced vets would have no such hesitation. One vet once confessed to me of "compassion fatigue".

Two incidents stand out for me. One was a young male cat who had been run over and had a fractured pelvis and breaks in both hind legs. It wasn't neutered and really needed referral to a specialist. The owners couldn't afford any treatment and no charity had the money to take on the case so the cat was euthanised despite the fact it could have been repaired and have led a normal life. I secretly wished that I had the money to pay for its treatment.

The other case was a young male cross Doberman who had allegedly bitten a child badly on the hand and was bought in to be put to sleep at the owner's request. Two young men brought it in with an ill-fitting muzzle on its nose. I could see that the dog was petrified. There was fear and bewilderment in its eyes. The child who had been bitten was smirking behind them, a couple of plasters on his left hand. The men didn't want to stay but signed the consent form and left. The dog had had no "trial" and as it lay dead on the consulting room floor, I wondered who would fight for animals that were abused far worse by their owners.

I started paying attention in class, especially in the sciences and my marks improved drastically. My parents were unaware as they never came to any parent-teacher evenings. I researched all about veterinary schools and the minimum qualifications needed to attend. My form master helped me decide my best options and was happy to support my application.

I developed an interest in drugs and medicines. The vets were always keen to show off their knowledge and expand mine. During my "A" levels, my grandfather suffered from an aggressive form of prostate cancer. I looked in fascination at the variety of drugs that were pumped into him before he died. He had tablets, intravenous injections and various potions he had to swallow. None seem to do any good except the morphine which make him very sleepy. When he died, Nana was left on her own in their big house. She was the only member of my family who showed any interest in me so I used to cycle up to see her regularly. As a reward for my twentieth birthday, she gave me Granddad's VW Polo. My parents hardly ever went to see her and she was always grateful for my visits.

I loved going up to the house; it was full pictures and carvings from Southern Africa. Grandfather had worked on the railways before Rhodesia became Zimbabwe. They went briefly to South Africa, but I think both my grandparents felt that my mother would be better off finishing her education back in England.

At Christmas and birthdays, grandma always gave me cash. I had told her of my ambition to get into vet school and had she encouraged it both verbally and financially. Although I had to study long and hard, I still visited her when I could. She was my family and loved reminiscing about her time in Southern Africa. I enjoyed her stories even though I heard the same story many times. She made Africa come to life and I knew one day I would travel there.

I took up bridge at university; a fourth was always in demand. At first, I struggled but soon I learnt that I could easily work out where all the cards were. I expect that I got that skill from my father. I gradually mastered the subtle art of letting my partner think it was their skill and not mine that won the rubber. Playing bridge also taught me how to read people.

As a student I needed to see as much practice as I could. The vet schools wanted me to get as much experience as I could with all different species. The practice still did a little horse work I was always keen to see any interesting cases. One Saturday afternoon the vet called me to say there was a badly injured pony in the woods. It was one of the new graduate assistants. I hurried around to the practice and I jumped into the back of the car with the duty vet and nurse. We got as close as we could then walked the rest of the way down a muddy track.

As a precaution, the vet took the humane killer with him together with a bag of dressings and drugs. But I wasn't sure if he knew how to use it. We could see at once that the pony was in agony. The owner had said it had been spooked by some dogs and had careered into a tree stump. There were chestnut hairs and blood left on a broken branch. His left humerus was shattered and was totally unrepairable. Bits of bone peered through the torn muscle in a gaping wound. There was surprisingly little blood. The pony's nostrils were flared and his back legs were flexed as he tried to take his weight on them.

I went around to the front of the pony. It was Buster. He recognised me immediately. I could see the pain and terror in his eyes. I felt helpless. I could feel him pleading with me to do something. The owner was distraught. The vet was rummaging around, looking dressings and for injections muttering to himself. He obviously hadn't a clue what to do. The owner was the woman in the purple jodhpurs from the stables. I could see that she recognised me. I got the nurse to hold Buster and took the gun out of the vet's bag. I flicked off the safety catch and checked there was a bullet ready to fire. I couldn't stand to see him suffer any longer.

He was making a pitiful whinnying noise that really got to me. I lined up the gun in the middle of his blazed forehead as I had been taught. He looked at me, pleading for me to end his suffering. I shut my eyes and pulled the trigger.

There was a big bang and Buster dropped to the ground and a little blood trickled out of his nostrils. It was over in an instant. Buster was no longer in agony. His eyes glazed over and the owner came over to thank me. She put her arms around me.

'Thank you. Thank you. He was in so much pain. You must really love animals to do that.' She sobbed into my shoulder.

The vet had a look of surprise on his face and he quickly put down the injection and dressing he was holding. He was about to say something then thought better of it.

As we walked back to the car, the nurse broke the silence, 'That pony was in agony. Thank god you shot it.'

The next day, the head nurse told me that the senior partner wanted to see me in his office. I knocked on the door and was told to come in. He was sitting at his desk on the phone and motioned me to sit down.

'Yes I see. Well, thank you. Yes, I will pass on your thanks, Mrs Williams. Goodbye.'

He put the phone down and swivelled in his chair to face me.

'I should, by rights, be telling you to pack your bags and not come back. But that was Mrs Williams who owned Buster and I have also spoken to the veterinary nurse who went on the visit with you yesterday. Both seem to think that you did the right thing. Indeed, Mrs Williams speaks very highly of you. The abattoir confirmed that Buster had a shattered humerus that would have been inoperable. He must have been in agony. Whilst I appreciate your good intentions, you can't just use a gun like that, especially when you don't have a licence. Where did you learn to shoot anyway? The nurse said it was perfectly placed.'

'I learnt to shoot at school,' I replied. 'We had rifles and pistols. It was one of the few things I was good at. We had a lecture at vet school last term with a demonstration.'

The senior partner looked at me. 'Hmm. I've spoken to the assistant, who wasn't very happy at all. But it would appear what you did was in the animal's best interest. That's what being a vet is all about: putting the animal first. Well, we won't say any more about it.'

I left the room. I never forgot what the senior partner said: putting the animal first. Of all the animals I ever put to sleep, the last moments with Buster with me will stay with me for the rest of my life.

I passed my veterinary exams with ease and was offered a job at my home practice. They were planning to move the practice to new purpose-built premises and concentrating on small animals. I continued to live at home but hardly saw my parents. But I did pay my mother rent every month, which she spent on booze.

One of the older receptionists invited me around to her house for Sunday lunch and introduced me to her daughter Meg. Her real name was Patricia Megan but every one called her Meg and she hated it if anyone ever called her Patricia. At first, we said nothing to each other but as the meal progressed we started talking and realised that we had a lot in common. Over the next few months, Meg and I saw a lot of each other when my rota allowed it. Inevitably one thing led to another and we became engaged.

I helped clear out the old practice and found a Gladstone bag in an old wardrobe. It had belonged to one of the original partners.

The vets laughed when I asked to keep it.

I took it home and forgot about it until one rainy day off when I was bored I undid it and peered inside.

There was a very old-fashioned stethoscope, a couple of small plastic syringes and two white polystyrene boxes. I took one out and shook it. There seemed to be something inside.

I pulled the two halves apart inside there were two large bottles of different coloured liquids and a small vial of a clear solution. One of the bottles contained a yellow liquid and was labelled "large animal Immobilon" and the other a blue solution labelled "large animal Revivon". The small vial was labelled "Narcan". They didn't look like they had been used. The other polystyrene box was the same.

I hadn't heard of the drug but looked it up in my formulary. It was an equine anaesthetic; one of the ingredients was a powerful morphine derivative that was potentially fatal in man. The antidote for accidental human injection was in the small bottle: naloxone. Apparently it could be absorbed through the eyes or by ingesting. In man, it could cause respiratory failure, cardiac arrest and death.

It wasn't a drug I would want to use; it sounded dangerous. I thought about throwing the drugs away and then thought better of it and put them back in the Gladstone bag.

I took Meg to see Nana and told her we were getting married. She insisted on giving us £10,000 to go towards a house. I couldn't believe it. But with my recent pay rise, savings and this money, we could buy our own flat.

She asked about work and how I felt about euthanasia.

I explained that it was part of our work and if an animal was suffering and beyond saving then it was the kindest solution.

'If I'm in that situation, I think that I would like that option.' She smiled at me but I knew she was being serious. 'Would you give me an injection if I asked you to?'

She looked at me straight into my eyes. I nodded very slightly.

'Good. I may hold you to that.'

I started expanding my drug collection in the Gladstone bag. Why; I don't know. It seemed fun. I added morphine, phenobarbitone, pentobarbitone, diazepam, digitalis and I even managed to find some out of date chloroform in an outhouse. It still smelt like it would work.

I started trying drugs on myself. Just in small quantities. It was interesting trying to dissolve the tablets. There was always some tablet residue left floating on top. I started premixing the tablets and filtering the liquid through coffee filter paper. This was a total failure. Then I used a sample bottle and siphoned off the liquid beneath the dusty meniscus using a syringe and long needle. It seemed to work and the drugs still had an effect on me. I realised if I repeated it using the same solution I could produce a highly concentrated drug mixture.

Diazepam was like being wrapped in a warm blanket that you snuggled down in and gently went to sleep.

Phenobarbitone was like someone suddenly turned out the lights. Tramadol sent me to sleep but I had weird and vivid dreams. I didn't like it.

I tried all three once. I went to sleep wearing my pyjamas in my bed and woke up fifteen hours later naked on the sofa with someone from work banging on the front door asking if I was alright as I was late for work. I can't remember anything about those fifteen hours, and I never repeated it.

Work was always busy but I always found time to visit Nana.

She started forgetting things. Carers were hired to come in during the day. She lost weight and lost confidence to go out. I still went to visit her with a takeaway but she tired quickly and she was no longer able to go upstairs so a bed was installed in her dining room. Luckily, there was a shower room downstairs. She developed an uncontrolled twitch and started having problems feeding herself.

There were times when she forgot to turn kitchen appliances off. The doctor came around and changed her medication and she seemed to perk up. But it was short-lived. She had problems breathing and her legs swelled up.

The wedding was a very quiet affair and straight afterwards, Meg and I moved into our new flat. I couldn't have been happier. We took the photos and video round to Nana which she seemed to enjoy but she couldn't remember who Meg was.

It wasn't long before she had a bad fall and was taken to hospital. When I got there, she was in a private room looking very small and pale in the bed. One side of her face was badly bruised and she was struggling for breath.

She smiled when she saw me and called me over.

'They want to put me in a home. I don't want to go.' She paused, sucking air into her lungs; then beckoned me closer with her finger. 'Don't get old. I've seen it happen to my friends. If I can't go back home, then I want to go, you know, up there.' She hesitated and then winked at me. 'Or down there.' She looked straight at me. I could see the pleading in her eyes. It was the most coherent she had been for a long time. I knew that it was taking all of her strength. But she was determined to finish saying what she wanted to. 'I want you to do to me what you do to old animals. Like we agreed.'

I looked at her quizzically. I could hardly hear what she was saying.

'You know when they can't walk or are incontinent. I want to go when I want to go. I want you to come back tomorrow. You can give me an injection and then read to me.'

'Are you sure?' I asked.

'Of course I'm sure. I've had a good life. Shame about my daughter. But you're settled with a nice wife. I'm tired. I hate the constant pain and I'm fed up with a body that doesn't work. Come back tomorrow with what you need.' She smiled at me then closed her eyes. She had managed to say what she had wanted to say. She was holding me to my promise.

The next day, I returned with two syringes pre-loaded with morphine. I spent some time deciding on which drug; pentobarbitone was what we used in animals but I felt that an over dose of morphine was less likely to cause alarm. They had given my grandfather loads of it before he had died. I wasn't sure of the dose but the two syringes were much more than I would give to a big dog.

A nurse nodded at me and smiled as I entered the room. Nana was sleeping. I turned to leave.

'No, you don't. I was just trying to remember when I was your age. Pull up a chair. What book have you bought?'

'*King Solomon's Mines*,' I replied. She would read it to me when I stayed over. She said it reminded her of her time in Zimbabwe. Or Rhodesia, as she used to call it.

There was a slight nod of her head and she settled back into her pillows. She sighed then gripped my wrist.

'Have you bought it?' I nodded in reply. 'Good. I told the doctor I was in a lot of pain and they gave some morphine earlier. I'm ready. Give it to me now.'

I took out one of the pre-loaded syringes took the cap off the needle and injected the liquid slowly into the fluid bag. When I had finished, I did the same with the other.

I put the empty syringes into my pocket; pulled out a well-thumbed book and started reading. As Nana drifted away, I could imagine her with Macumazahn, Bougwan and Incubu on the Southern African high veldt.

After an hour, her breathing shallowed so much I could hardly see her chest move. It was time to go. I put away my book. Put on my coat and left.

'She seems very sleepy,' I said to a nurse and left.

My father told me of Nana's death the next morning. Natural causes seemed to be the diagnosis. I heard pneumonia mentioned and the body was fairly quickly released for cremation—much to my relief.

We went to the funeral but couldn't go to the wake. Meg had started losing the feeling in one of her arms and we had an appointment with a consultant.

A couple of days later I had a phone call from my father asking me to call round. When I got home, my mother was in a terrible state.

'She's left it all to him. We can live off the interest of the investments but he gets the capital after I die.' She pointed accusingly at me.

I walked into the kitchen where my parents were standing.

'What do you mean?' I asked.

'My mother has left all her money and investments to you including the house. Your father and I can have the interest from her investments to live off whilst I am alive but we can't sell anything. I've just come from the solicitor's now. How did you do it?' She glared at me, refilled her glass and stormed upstairs.

My father stared at me, then lowered his eyes, picked up his keys and left the house. No doubt to play poker.

I felt no guilt on Nana's death. She was in a better place now. But Meg was worrying me. We had to go up to London to see a specialist neurologist. But it didn't look good for her.

Meg

The specialist in London wasn't very positive. Meg had more blood tests, a brain scan and they tested her muscles. Motor neurone disease was a tentative diagnosis as her grandmother had had frontotemporal dementia. Meg was distraught. We hadn't talked about children but I knew that someday she wanted to have them. Private specialists in America were mentioned but we didn't have the money. Although I knew I would have the necessary funds when my mother died.

That thought stuck with me. I didn't see her very often but I knew she was drinking even more now. Her face was lined and blotchy. Her youthful good looks gone and there were no admirers now. My father played poker most of the weekend and so my mother was left watching television with a liquid supper.

I started driving around to their house on a Friday night and watched the routine. I told Meg that I was working. My father would get in from work at 5.00pm. He would get changed then make himself a cup of tea and a sandwich. At 7.00pm, he would leave the house. As far as I could tell, he would return at about 4.00am.

On Saturday mornings, they would both emerge at about 10.30am in their dressing gowns: my mother puffing on a cigarette and my father drinking a mug of coffee. They would leave the house at midday when they would go to the supermarket for the weekly shop. My mother had lost her driving licence so my father provided this favour. In the afternoon, my father would watch sport and my mother would nurse a bottle of wine in the kitchen. There would be a shouting match at about 7.00 o'clock in the evening and my father would leave only to return early on Sunday morning. My mother would go upstairs for a bath then come downstairs at about 8.00 to watch Saturday night TV in the company of a wine box.

I didn't bother to check the Sunday routine. I had a plan for Saturday night.

We had one assistant who was very keen on performing glucose curves on diabetic animals. She had made a name for herself at stabilising difficult cases and had attracted many of the diabetic animals from other practices. As a result, we always had a large stock of soluble insulin and animals requiring regular blood samples.

The Saturday I chose was no exception. There were two dogs in for glucose curves. The rest of the animal hospital was quiet; there were just a couple of stray cats. I had managed to find a half empty box of 5mg diazepam in the charity medicines which I put in my pocket. At 6.30pm, I told the duty nurse I would monitor the dogs for the next hour and a half, she could go home and get something to eat.

As soon as she had gone, I grabbed a couple of disposable gloves, a tourniquet, a bottle of soluble insulin and a two ml syringe. I had already dissolved four of the diazepam tablets and they were in a small pot in my pocket. I wasn't going to mess around with insulin syringes and needles. There was no car in the driveway so my father had already left. I could hear my mother in the kitchen pouring a glass of wine. She put the bottle back into the fridge and went into the lounge.

I put on the gloves and went into the kitchen and she turned the TV over to a games show and turned up the volume. I opened the fridge and took out the bottle. It was 2/3rds empty so she was on her second glass. I emptied the contents of the pot in my pocket into the bottle and gently shook it. The yellow liquid seemed to disperse into the wine.

I slowly crept upstairs waited in my father's bedroom after putting the rest of the diazepam tablets in the bathroom cabinet. It wasn't long before my mother returned for the rest of the bottle. I looked down at her from the top of the stairs. She emptied the bottle into her glass then tipped the bottle into her mouth to catch the dregs. After about a quarter of an hour, I could hear her coming up stairs. The combination of wine and diazepam were having their effect. She had to use both hands on the banisters.

As she reached the top step, I sprang out at her, shouting and waving my arms over my head. As predicted, she fell back in surprise and tumbled head over heels down the wooden staircase and her head hit the solid hall floor with a resounding thud. I rushed down the stairs after her. Her eyes were shut and there was some bleeding coming from the back of her head. I pulled up the dress sleeve on her left arm. Her arm felt limp. I fastened the tourniquet around her arm and raised her vein. I put the insulin bottle into my mouth and filled the 2ml syringe. This would be a massive overdose but I was banking on accidental death being the obvious conclusion. As I injected the insulin, she opened her eyes. At first, she didn't recognise me. The confusion turned to hate and she spat in my face.

'Just so you know,' I said to her softly, removing the syringe and wiping my face. 'I killed your daughter, and I killed your mother, and now I'm killing you.'

But her eyes showed no emotion and her body started convulsing. The hypoglycaemia was starting to have an effect. It was time to go.

When I got back to the practice, I did the two blood tests and entered the results on the sheets hanging on the cage, making sure I put down the time I was at my parents' house. The nurse returned and I stayed until 10.00pm before returning home to Meg.

She was already asleep. Soon we would have the money to pay for any treatment Meg needed.

I slept through the phone calls my father made during the early hours of the morning and as it was a Sunday morning, we didn't get up until at least 9.30 in the morning.

The kettle was boiling when he banged on the door. I let him in. It was obvious he hadn't slept. His eyes were puffy and his thinning hair un-brushed.

'It's your mother. There's been an accident. She's fallen down the stairs and had some sort of stroke.' He took a deep breath and wiped his nose with his sleeve. 'She's dead.'

I heaved a sigh of relief.

'I'm sorry, Dad.' I put an arm on his shoulder. 'What happened?'

'You know she was drinking heavily. Well I think she was taken anti-depressants as well. She went upstairs for a bath and she must have fallen and hit her head on the floor. That's what the paramedic thought when they came to pick up the body. I didn't get in until 4.00. They thought she had been there for a good eight hours.'

I tried to comfort him as best I could. I didn't think he would have been so upset.

Everyone agreed that it had been a tragic accident and after the funeral and cremation, my father and I sat alone in the sitting room.

'What will you do now?' I asked him. I had thought about putting my arm on his shoulder as a gesture of comfort but couldn't bring myself to do it.

My father sniffed and wiped his nose.

'I can't stay here. I'm making more money from poker than at work. I'll probably sell up and move to a flat nearer London.'

I nodded. At least, he hadn't asked me for money.

'Dad. I have to get back to Meg. Keep in touch.'

My father looked at me, shook my hand and smiled. 'Yes I'd like that.'

I took one last look at the lounge left. That was the last time I saw or spoke to him.

Now I had Nana's money, I took Meg to see a specialist in London. She had started having problems swallowing and was slurring some of her words. The doctors repeated all the previous tests and gave Meg a CT scan. The results weren't good. The type of motor neurone disease she had was untreatable and progressive.

When we got home, Meg wanted to go to the local café where we had done a lot of our courting.

'I don't think that I can do this.' She tried to sip her tea but she could hardly swallow. 'What would you do if I was an animal? I want you to help me. I'll write a note explaining everything. It will be my decision. Mine alone.'

I begged her not to talk about it but I could see she had made up her mind. The doctor's grim prognosis had persuaded her.

She was the only person I had ever loved. How could I do this? How could I not?

She discussed what she wanted to do: the when and the where. I realised this had been playing on her mind for some time.

Over the next few days, I assembled all I needed from the practice.

On the Sunday morning, we made love for the last time. She sat in her favourite chair in the lounge. I set up the drip into her arm and we opened a decent bottle of vintage claret. She had found it too difficult to swallow Champagne.

She had decided what film she wanted to watch and I loaded the DVD player.

As I put three preloaded syringes on the coffee table beside her, she put her hand on my gloved hand.

'I love you. Now go to work. You mustn't be implicated in any way.' She reached under her chair and pulled out an envelope.

'It's all in here. It's my decision. Mine alone. I've said I hadn't been drinking enough water so you helped with the drip to prevent dehydration. Now go.'

I kissed her on her forehead. I thought I would cry but no tears came. I suppose my emotions were buried so deep nothing could release them.

Music erupted from the TV; the film had started. It was a romcom I had never watched.

When I got to the door, I took one last look at my wife, she was looking intently at the film. Then I turned and went to work. I didn't feel sad or upset, just relieved that she wouldn't suffer anymore. Not many people get to choose how and when they die. I have every intention that I will.

We had arranged for Meg's mother to find her. She often helped with the cleaning so had a key.

I was still at work when the call came through. The paramedics had taken her to the hospital and I met Meg's mother there. Her eyes were puffed with tears and she looked at me with suspicion. But she held her tongue. The letter was accepted in view of her condition and I had a very brief interview with the police. They assumed that Meg had taken the drugs herself from the practice as she often helped me out of hours.

Her body was released and she was cremated three weeks after her death. I wasn't sure what to do with her ashes so I had them buried with Nana's.

I was now a wealthy man, certainly by vet standards. I got house clearance in and sold Nana's house without going back to it. I sold the flat and bought a small house on the edge of town. The rest of the money I invested in the stock market, predominantly in income shares. The practice let me cut down my hours whilst I decided what to do. The clients thought I was a better vet than I really was and I had developed a loyal following among the older, wealthier clients so the practice was keen to keep me on. I worked four afternoons and evenings shifts a week giving me ample time to plan my future.

Every morning, I would sit at the café were Meg and I would discuss our future. There I would have breakfast and watch the world go by from my window seat at the table the owner reserved for me every morning. It wasn't for sentimental reasons but because they had molasses matured bacon from a local pig farm. It was the best bacon I had ever tasted and they used to crisp it up for me just how I liked it.

Post-Mortem

The boat was nearing the marina. I put down my tea and judged the tide. According to the tables, it should be high tide now but the moored boats were still parallel to the shore, so the tide was still coming in but some of the heavier boats nearer the bank were starting to turn as the current lessened.

It was a still cloudless, star-filled sky and I could see the entrance to the marina. The water was dull black in the shadow of the moored boats.

A couple of the houseboats had lights on and music was drifting up from one, gentle classical music. Mozart, I think.

I had to concentrate on steering the boat, the mooring was at ninety degrees to the river and any tide would push the bow.

I judged my angle, revved the engine at little to gain headway then turned it off to let the boat glide into its birth.

A gentle bump told me the boat was in as far as it could go and I jumped over the side onto the pontoon to secure a line.

Once the boat was secure, I went down into the cabin to clear up. I always liked a tidy ship. I put the mug away, emptied the kettle and put the box of teabags back into the cupboard. By some soup packets, there was a bottle of ketchup I don't think I had ever used.

Ketchup always reminded me of my first act of animal revenge after Meg's death.

I made sure that the boat was safely locked up. It was nearly time to take the boat out of the water for the annual service, clean and anti-foul.

Mr Tibbles and I drove home. It was late and I had a lot to do tomorrow.

Ketchup

Meg had been gone about six months. I had sorted my affairs and established a gentle routine that I enjoyed. I would go to the café for breakfast and read the newspaper. People were so used to seeing me, I became invisible. After breakfast, I took a brisk walk along the side roads, through the park and back to the flat.

I had a very light lunch and would arrive at the practice for afternoon surgery for two hours. Then a short break before evening surgery then back home for TV or a book, supper and bed. I played bridge once a fortnight with a small group of professionals—teachers, doctors, etc., which I enjoyed. It was entertaining listening to their gossip.

It sounds boring, I know. But it was just what I needed; routine stability. But the fates had other ideas.

One quiet weekday evening, just after 5pm, a distraught elderly woman brought in a young dark tabby cat called Ted. He was bleeding from a wound in his back right leg. At first, I thought it was a bite wound but further inspection showed it typical of a bullet wound. Some of his hair had been pulled in to the wound by the force of the bullet.

X-rays showed not one but three bullets imbedded in the cat's muscle. The owner was understandably distressed.

Whilst I removed the bullets, the receptionist telephoned the police who had zero interest in the case. We had better luck with the RSPCA. But unless the culprit was caught in the act, there was nothing anyone would do.

Ted was a really nice cat who purred gently when I stroked his chin as he came around from the anaesthetic.

He deserved revenge, but he had no means of achieving it. I would act on his behalf.

I went to visit the owner when I took out Ted's sutures. She lived in a small south-facing bungalow with an immaculate garden. I could see where Ted would lie in the sun next to a small garden shed. After closer inspection, I found a couple of spots of blood. I lay on the ground and peered up as if I was Ted. There were three flats opposite where the pellets could have come from. I looked inside the garden shed. It was full of pots and garden implements but there was just enough room to sit by the window and observe the three flats.

The owner was convinced Ted had only just been shot when she bought him in.

That suggested maybe it was someone after school.

I took a week's holiday and parked my car opposite the flats and watched.

As the days went by, I worked out who lived where and there was one boy who was my main suspect. He was a weedy-looking red-headed boy that I used to see sometimes walk past the café in the morning on Saturday mornings. But I really needed proof.

The practice kept any stray cats that had been found dead such as a road traffic accident in the body freezer at the back of the practice for at least a month in case the owner came forward.

I went into the practice and had a look in the freezer. There was a young black male cat. It was a stray that had been brought in a few days earlier. It would do.

I took him home and thawed him out overnight.

After lunch, I went around to Tom's owner and explained what I was going to do. The weather was perfect. At first, she was reluctant but when I told her that the cat was dead and would have a "special" cremation, she was happy.

I arranged the black cat as if it was sleeping and took my position in the shed. I knew nothing would happen until schools were let out, so I read a book.

The noise in the street told me it was time to put the book away and watch the flat windows. I had a rough idea where the boy lived.

Nothing. At six o'clock, I left the shed, put the cat in a black sack and went home.

It was the same the next day.

But on the third day, just when I was about to leave, I saw a bedroom window open and a gun barrel and peering down it was the red-headed boy.

I heard a small thud and then the window closed.

I took the black cat home and labelled it for a private cremation. It was the least I could do.

The next Saturday, I followed the boy after he passed the café. He went to the public basketball court and played there for an hour with some other boys before going on his own to the cafe. He had a burger and fries before returning home. All the boys had their own water bottles which they left on a bench outside the court. The inklings of an idea began to crystallise in my head.

All the tables at the café had small bottles of ketchup on them and I noticed that Jimmy, I discovered that was his name, got through half a bottle.

At the vets, we were always culturing bacteria from different samples including faeces. E. Coli was a common finding and suited my needs. It would cause a nasty, but not fatal, gastroenteritis in Jimmy.

I took a full ketchup bottle I had taken from the café, emptied out half of the contents, and mixed as much of the bacteria as I could scrap off a Petrie dish with the ketchup then replaced it in the bottle.

The next Saturday I watched from my car Jimmy as walked past the café on his way to the basketball court. He had the same blue water container he always took. I waited for half an hour then went to the basketball court. I had told the café owner I would have lunch there for a change.

The boys were all concentrating on playing so no-one noticed me put some frusemide in Jimmy's bottle. I went home, parked the car and walked to the café where I sat at my usual table to have a sandwich and a cup of tea.

Jimmy came in looking hot and sweaty and drunk greedily from his water bottle. He had just put in his order when the frusemide kicked in and he got up to go to the toilet.

I got up, carefully leaving my newspaper on the chair. I switched the ketchup bottle on his table with the spiked one in my pocket, paid my bill and left just as Jimmy returned. I could see through the window him dousing everything with ketchup then stuffing it in his mouth.

Half an hour later I went back to the café. Jimmy had already gone. I switched ketchup bottles back again, retrieved my paper and went home.

It was two weeks later that I discovered the true extent of what had happened when I was playing bridge with a couple of teachers and a doctor. On the Monday morning, Jimmy's mother had phoned him in sick. But his gastroenteritis had been very bad and he had got so dehydrated he had to be admitted to hospital for IV fluids and antibiotics. He had to stay in hospital for three days before they allowed him home.

The hospital had grown E.coli in their laboratory and sent environmental health around to the café. But they found nothing suspicious.

I asked where they thought the infection had come from and it was thought he must have picked it up from some infected dog faeces on the basketball court.

I sent Jimmy an anonymous note saying if he shot any more cats, he would get something far worse.

I saw Ted and his owner three months later for his annual vaccination. I persuaded his owner to let me x-ray him. There were no more pellets so it looked like Jimmy had heeded my warning. But I did notice the council put up a notice outside the basketball court declaring "NO DOGS".

Castration

Every Friday morning, whilst I ate my breakfast at the café, I noticed an old woman wheeling a tartan shopping trolley down to the shops. Half an hour later, she would struggle back with it, laden with her shopping.

I knew her because every six weeks, she brought her budgie "Billy" to have its beak and nails clipped. I remember being told to clip the nails before the beak otherwise the budgie will nip you. She usually saw the senior partner but when he was off, she consented to see me. It was only after several visits that I noticed from the records she had had several budgerigars that were all called "Billy".

One Friday her way back from the shops, a youth on a moped knocked into her, sending her and her shopping flying. I ran out of the café and helped her to her feet. A couple of passers-by helped load her shopping trolley.

She thanked us, confirmed she wasn't hurt and continued on her way.

The next Friday, the same thing happened.

I saw the youth on the moped before he hit the old lady and quickly wrote down the number beside the half-finished crossword.

I could see that the old lady was badly shaken this time. She couldn't stop shaking and there was real fear in her eyes.

I walked her home and sat her down in her front room with a cup of tea. She was adamant she didn't want to pursue the youth on the moped. I think she was frightened they would come after her if she pressed charges. I noticed she had some bowls of food on the kitchen floor.

'That's for Mr Tibbles.' I think she could see a puzzled look on my face. 'He's a stray cat I feed. He seems to eat anything. If I'm lucky, he'll come on my lap in the evening.'

As I left the house, I could see a large black and white cat looking at me from under a bush. He blinked and came over, rubbing himself on my legs. He had the bushiest tail I had ever seen.

'You must be Mr Tibbles.' I stroked the cat on his head. He purred loudly, sniffed my trousers then returned to his spot under the bush.

I didn't see the woman for a month until I was asked to do a house visit to clip the budgie's nails.

When I got to the house, it was in a dreadful state. It hadn't been cleaned for weeks and the budgie's cage was a terrible mess. I cleaned out Billy's cage, gave him fresh water and seed and clipped his claws and beak. I made us both a cup of tea and sat down with her in the front room.

The woman had lost weight; she looked drawn and old.

Suddenly, I felt a weight descend on my lap. It was Mr Tibbles. She smiled at me. It was a tired half smile. 'You're privileged. You're the first person he has done that to apart from me.'

I had to do something. I still remembered the moped license plate. As I left, I turned to her. 'Are you sure you don't want to pursue it?'

She shook her head.

Well. I would on her behalf.

It was approaching summer and on the light evenings, teenagers would often congregate down the seafront to pose and drive up and down. The youth was there, he was obviously well known and he was laughing and joking with some others, smoking dope. After a couple of hours, they started to get bored and drifted away. I followed him home.

I discovered that he lived in a rough area of town with his mother. There was no sign of anyone else living with them. His mother worked long shifts at the local supermarket, especially on Saturdays when she would take her bicycle out of the garage and cycle to work. He son would emerge at about 11.00am, get out his moped and drive to a pub on the high street.

As no-one had died, I didn't want to kill him. Just give him a harsh lesson. I had seen a pair of emasculators at work. That would do. After all, we castrated feral cats before releasing them.

I went around to see the old lady but there was a 'for sale' sign outside the house. A neighbour told me that she had been put into a home and her house had been put on the market. I found Mr Tibbles under his bush. He meowed and came over purring, weaving in and out of my legs. I didn't have any option but to take him home with me.

Mr Tibbles settled in as soon as he arrived home. I went down to the local pet shop and bought all I thought he would need and then started to plan his owner's revenge.

Saturday morning would be the time. I told work I was going to put flowers on Meg and Nana's ashes in the churchyard.

I watched the mother leave the house then went to a florist near home to buy some flowers, trying to make sure they would remember me. The night before, I had put all I needed into the back of my car. I had chloroform, some alcohol, local anaesthetic, a couple of scalpel blades in a sterilised stitch-up kit and the horse emasculators. They had been sterilised over a year ago but they should still be alright. There was the date they had last been sterilised on the autoclave tape. I had carefully removed them so I could reuse the autoclave bag.

I put on some gloves and eased into the garage about 10.30. There was no-one else around. I could hear the youth in the kitchen next door. There a small space behind the kitchen door and I waited there with a large wad of cotton wool and the bottle of chloroform. The door blasted open and the youth strode through. I pressed the chloroform over the youth's mouth and nose and he crumpled to the floor. I turned him on his back and put a surgical mask on his face and saturated it in chloroform. I pulled off his trousers: he wasn't wearing any underpants. There wasn't enough hair to worry about clipping so I poured the alcohol over his scrotum. The skin shrunk, identifying the two testicles.

I put a fenestrated drape over the operation site and I injected both testicles with a couple of mls of local anaesthetic and put a bleb under the skin where I would incise.

I griped one of the testicles and incised into it. There was a small line of blood along the incision; I squeezed and the testicle popped through the hole in the scrotum, covered in the tunica. I cut through this and teased out the testicle, freed it from connective tissue and reached for the emasculators. I was just about to clamp them shut when I realised I had them the wrong way round, "nut to nut" was the expression I had learnt as a student. I turned the emasculators around, clamped them around the cord and pulled the handles shut as hard as I could. My hand was only just big enough. I could hear the flesh being crushed. The youth's body twitched but he stayed asleep. I clamped the small blood vessel, poured some more chloroform on the mask and repeated the procedure on the other testicle.

There was surprisingly little blood. I cleaned the whole area with a swab soaked in alcohol and wrapped everything, including the testicles, in the drape.

What I didn't see was the small sterilisation indicator strip parachute down from the suture kit and slide underneath some old boxes out of sight.

I put his trousers back on again, took off the mask and left.

There was no-one about and I drove back to the graveyard and put some flowers on both the gravestones.

That afternoon, I cleaned and replaced the emasculators in their old autoclave bag; I nearly put the testicles in the clinical waste but decided against it. I would take them home with me. I left the kit for the nurses to deal with.

Mr Tibbles was waiting for me when I got home. I went into the kitchen, turned the hob on and got out a saucepan. I thinly sliced the testicles and sautéed them with some garlic, olive oil and at the last moment added a few prawns.

When it had cooled, I put it into Mr Tibbles's bowl. He sniffed it then wolfed it down, licked his lips and looked up at me as if asking for more, before settling himself down in my armchair for an after lunch nap.

Immediately afterwards, I didn't hear much more about it. The police came around to the surgery and one of the nurses showed a bemused PC around the prep room and the sterilised instruments. I got the impression he had been asked to go around to all the local vets. I watched him surreptitiously; he had a cursory look at the emasculators, checked the date and moved on.

When I was playing bridge two weeks later, one of the players was a hospital administrator who had been in A&E the afternoon of the castration.

The youth had been brought in by his distraught mother. The doctor confirmed the surgical castration but could offer no clue as to the perpetrator. The mother was shouting and screaming, demanding justice.

I thought that would be the end of it. How wrong I was.

Overdose

One of my bridge partners was a GP who had deliberately found a job near the sea so he could indulge in his passion for sailing. Without telling his wife, he had spent a small fortune buying a 33-foot day cruiser and had arranging mooring at the local marina. Unfortunately, his wife, a nurse quite a few years younger than him, wasn't impressed.

He didn't tell his wife till after he had bought it and before it was delivered. According to the doctor, she was full of enthusiastic ignorance until the boat arrived. I think she had thought he had bought a motor cruiser rather than a sailing yacht and had visions of entertaining her friends and motoring up the coast.

To give her credit, she had tried to help out as crew but it hadn't worked. She hated it when the boat tilted and clung on in the hatchway, shouting expletives. One evening after bridge, the doctor approached me as we packed up and asked if I wanted to try sailing. I thought for a minute then I agreed to have a go.

I loved it. The power of the tide and the wind fascinated me and I even started going to theory lessons at the local sailing club in the evenings. Most Sundays we would go out with our lunch on board and depending on the tides and wind, we would moor and eat on the boat or take the small tender to shore and have a picnic on the river bank. The weekends we didn't go out I would find myself at a loose end so would sit at the café longer than usual, reading the paper.

It was one wet Sunday morning; I was struggling with the crossword when I heard a yelp through the rain. I tried to look through the window but could see nothing.

I heard the yelp again, this time louder. Whoever was making the sound was not happy. I put down the newspaper, put on my raincoat and peered outside. I could just make out a staffie on the other side of the road. It was holding its paw up in pain but the owner kept pulling the dog by its lead and hitting it with a stick to make it move. He was a stout bearded man with long unkept hair, wearing an old parka jacket.

The dog had obviously damaged the paw and needed veterinary attention, not owner abuse.

I followed them up a muddy footpath to a rickety brown wooden gate. I looked through a hole in the fence; the dog was cowering whilst the man beat it again and again.

This was unusual as in my experience, most of the less well-off treasured the companionship of a dog and looked after it at their own expense.

The dog was left tied up in the rain and the man went inside.

I couldn't leave this alone.

I hurried back to my house, retrieved my Gladstone bag. When I got to the house, I saw a man leaving with sunglasses and a baseball cap. He was counting out some money which he thrust into his pocket. He got into a BMW with a flashy number plate and drove off.

The dog was still tied up outside in the rain.

I went through the gate. The dog looked quizzically at me so I gave it a couple of dog treats I had in my pocket and untied it so it could lie out of the rain.

I could see the yob through the kitchen window; he was sitting in old mock leather armchair smoking a joint. He was still wearing his coat, his beard and hair indistinguishable from the faux fur collar. The room was filthy with cartons and rubbish piled on the floor. There was an ashtray on the side of the chair laden with cigarette and joint butts. Despite the headphones he was wearing, I could still hear the music but I didn't recognise what it was. It just sounded like noise.

I put on some gloves and took out chloroform from the bag and soaked some cottonwool with it. Then put the bag down and went into the room. The man drew deeply on the joint then lay back in the chair. There was hardly any struggle as the chloroform took effect and he slumped forward, unconscious. I retrieved the bag, got out the morphine and filled up two syringes; a 5ml and a small 1ml. When I pulled up his sleeve, I could see needle marks in his veins. That would explain his behaviour to the dog.

I put on the tourniquet. Found an unbruised area, removed the tourniquet and injected the large syringe then the small syringe filled with morphine. I let the small syringe drop to the floor. It found a rare uncovered floorboard and the needle impaled in the stained wood. I left the tourniquet loose at his shoulder and put everything else back in the bag.

To me, it looked like a tragic drug overdose.

I looked around for some dog food. There wasn't any but I found some microwaveable meals in the fridge. They were a little out of date but I didn't think that the dog wound mind. I heated them in the microwave then emptied them in a bowl and gave the food to the dog, who couldn't have tasted any of it he wolfed it down so fast. I filled the bowl with water and gave it to him. He drank gratefully, slurping it onto the floor.

I went into the hall. There was a phone on the wall. I picked it up and listened; there was a dial tone, emergencies only. I dialled the police and told them there was an abandoned dog at this address then hung up before they could ask any more questions.

That should work even if it took a few hours. We are supposed to be a nation of animal lovers. The dog had been fed and watered and the ex-owner wouldn't trouble it any more. I found the gas meter, put some money in it and turned up the heating.

I picked up my bag and took one last look. The dog was dozing by a radiator. He looked up at me and wagged his tail. The druggie was laid back lifeless in the armchair, his arm draped over the arm, the empty syringe sticking like a dart in the floor.

I felt no remorse; the dog would be rehomed to someone who would care properly for it. The drug addict must have had a pitiful life living in such squalor and was probably better off. Certainly, society was.

A few days later, the dog was brought into the vets for a check-up before re-homing. He was already looking fatter and brighter. The RSPCA inspector said the police had been found him at a house where the owner died of a drug overdose. But they already had a new home lined up with a young couple who lived in a house the country with a large garden. They had decided to call him Billy after the police who "rescued him".

Shadow and Cody

I enjoyed working with the RSPCA inspectors. The other assistants didn't because there was no money in it for them. Occasionally, I went on visits with the inspectors to see for myself the appalling conditions some animals were kept in. Shortly after Billy was rehomed, I went with the inspector to see a woman who had been reported several times. It was claimed that she had several animals at her house that were neglected.

It was a nondescript terraced house in a rundown area of town. The small front garden was unkempt and the windows and front door were unpainted and dirty. The inspector tried the doorbell but there was no response; the batteries were probably dead. He banged loudly on the door and I could see several neighbours' curtains twitch.

Eventually, a large woman answered the door. She had badly dyed blond hair that was pulled into a ponytail. She had several piercings in her face and an indistinct tattoo on her left shoulder. Behind her, I saw a kitten flick its tail behind a door.

'What do you want?' She spat the words angrily at the inspector. She didn't seem to notice me.

The inspector showed the women his identity card.

'We've had several complaints from different sources that you have some animals here that are not being properly looked after.'

'Ain't no animals here,' the woman snapped back.

'Can we come in?' The inspector asked politely.

'No. I'm busy.' The woman slammed the door in our faces.

The inspector sighed. 'I'll have to get the police involved and get a warrant.'

A month later, we were back at the house with a policeman and a warrant. The woman tried to resist but in the end, she was forced to let us in.

Upstairs was an open hatch leading to the loft where some cats and kittens were being kept. There was insulation material everywhere and all the cats were scratching themselves and the kittens had runny eyes and some were sneezing incessantly.

In the kitchen were two dogs living in filth. There were black bags filled with rubbish everywhere. Dirty plates had been slung into the sink and there were empty takeaway cartons everywhere.

There was an elderly black Labrador, whom the owner called Shadow, who was lying amongst the bags. He was emaciated and had no hair down his back or legs. I could see fleas jumping around on his body. He didn't have the energy to wag his tail. His eyes were full of pain and misery.

The other dog was an equally emaciated white staffie called Cody. She was younger and seemed a little brighter. She was frantically foraging in the rubbish bags and takeaway cartons looking for food. She was crawling with fleas as well.

My body felt itchy just looking at the two dogs.

The woman showed no remorse or guilt. She swore at us constantly and spat at us as we left.

We loaded the animals into the RSPCA inspector's van and took them back to the surgery. I did a rough body scour; they were severely malnourished.

Two nurses and I spent about an hour combing through the dogs' and cats' coats. I wanted to get some idea how bad the flea infestation was.

We filled a phial with live fleas and their faeces to see how many there were. I thought about throwing it away but some instinct made me keep it. Lid tight shut, I popped it into my pocket.

The nurses gave the dogs a bath then treated them for fleas and worms.

However, it was obvious that Shadow was in a very bad way despite no complaints from him when we bathed and examined him. When he was still wet from his bath, I could see that his back and pelvis were very painful to move. There was severe urine scalding on his tummy where he had been lying in his own urine. There were deep ulcers over his hips that oozed blood and pus. Most of his teeth were missing and those that were left were covered in tartar and he had terrible halitosis. He must have been in constant pain from the arthritis and wounds and distressed from the overwhelming flea burden.

There was no doubt he was suffering terribly and was beyond getting better to be rehomed. The kindest course of action would be euthanasia which the inspector agreed. It was with a heavy heart that I gave him the injection. As I gave it to him, he looked up at me, the pain in his eyes easing as he slipped away. He didn't deserve this. It was if he was asking me to avenge him. She needed to be sorry for how she had made him suffer.

Cody was much younger and brighter and I could see that with good care and good food, she could be rehomed.

The cats were malnourished. There were two young mothers and their kittens. All the kittens had eye infections which we started treating after we gave them a bath. Unfortunately, a couple of the kittens would have permanent damage to their eyes. But that shouldn't affect their quality of life and kittens were always easy to re-home.

The RSPCA inspector asked me to make a written statement which would form the basis of the prosecution case.

When I asked what punishment she would get, the inspector thought for a minute. 'Maybe a ten-year ban on keeping animals.' He saw the look of disappointment on my face. 'If we are lucky. She hasn't any money so a fine is pointless.'

To me that didn't seem right. I had to do something for Shadow.

I started watching her house. She seemed to do the odd cleaning job and not much else but every Saturday night, she would get an Indian takeaway delivered to her house.

I spayed the two mother cats, unfortunately both were pregnant and I had the depressing task of killing the unborn kittens. That made me even more determined.

During the week when she was out, I went around the back of the house. The kitchen was more of a "lean-to" added on after the main house had been built. Whoever had done it hadn't done a very good job and the wooden back door was rotten and I could easily force the lock open. I could get inside when she answered the door for the curry delivery.

That Saturday, I waited in my car a little way down the street. As soon as the delivery arrived, I got out of the car. I heard the doorbell ring and a moment later, the woman answered the door and I barged the kitchen back door open.

I went out to collect the Gladstone bag and just managed to close the door as she came back into the kitchen, scouting around for a knife and fork in the debris in the kitchen sink.

She went back into the lounge and I cautiously reopened the door. I could hear a game show on the TV and the paper lids being ripped off the Indian takeaway.

She was oblivious to me as I reached into the bag, pulled out a wad of cotton wool and soaked it in chloroform. She struggled initially, scattering the dishes with her feet but she soon went quiet.

I needed her upstairs so I put my arms under her armpits and dragged her up the wooden stairs. Her ill-fitting tracksuit started sliding down her legs and as I reached the top of the stairs, they slid down.

I manhandled her onto the bed. She had thick white thighs covered in sores and I could see a ring of flea bites around her ankles. She would already be sensitised to flea bites. I went downstairs to retrieve the Gladstone bag, flicking the tracksuit trousers onto the sofa. I went back upstairs and rummaged inside the bag and found the phial of fleas I had removed from her pets. Carefully unscrewing it, I shook half the contents into her dyed blond hair and the rest I emptied down the front of her grey, mottled knickers.

I gave her an injection of diazepam to keep her quiet and went over to the loft hatch. I reached up and pulled down two large wads of insulation material which I shook over her bare legs. I needed something with a bit more weight to help hold her down on the bed. I didn't want to tie her down in case the ropes left suspicious marks on her legs. In the other bedroom amongst the rubbish, I found a couple of dilapidated suitcases that were very heavy. I hauled them into the bedroom and laid them on top of the woman's body and legs. I went into the bathroom, filled a dirty tooth mug with cold water. Then I went back into the bedroom and threw the water into the woman's face.

She awoke with a start but the diazepam and suitcases prevented her from doing anything more than screaming at me. There were a couple of sharp bangs on the wall from the house next door and a muffled voice telling us to be quiet. I took some tape from my pocket and wrapped it around her face, covering her mouth. She stared at me, hate in her eyes.

Then she started to itch; first her head, then her crotch and lastly her legs. The suitcases and the drugs prevented her from getting up. I pulled an injection of frusemide, a powerful diuretic, from the Gladstone bag and injected it into the woman's arm.

'Do you know who I am?' I asked the woman. She nodded then started scratching her head, her arms flopping in the air, not quite responding to her commands.

'Do you know why I am here?'

She shook her head vigorously, half in response to my question and half due to the fleas.

'I need you to feel guilty for how you treated Shadow and Cody.'

The woman looked confused then continued to try and scratch her head and groin. Her legs were twitching as the irritants from the insulation affected them.

'Want to know why you're so itchy? I put half the fleas we combed off your animals in your hair and the rest I tipped down your knickers.'

For the first time, the woman looked frightened.

'I've covered your legs with the insulation material your cats had to live in.'

I could see that the diazepam injection was starting to wear off so I gave her another. It wouldn't be long before the frusemide started to work.

I could see her shifting weight from one buttock to the other and her face started to redden. Then she couldn't hold it in any longer and she urinated on the bed. Her knickers streaked red as the urine soaked the bloody flea faeces.

'Shadow had to lie in his own urine. Not comfortable, is it?'

The woman didn't know what to do. She was itching everywhere and lying in her own urine. Her head and thighs were constantly twitching.

'Maybe now you can appreciate what Shadow had to suffer.'

The woman seemed to understand at last.

'I had to put Shadow to sleep because of your neglect.'

I could see the woman panic, she realised where this was going to lead.

I got a bottle of soluble insulin out of the Gladstone bag. It was still cold from when I had taken it out of the practice fridge earlier. I filled up a syringe and injected it into the woman's arm. It would only take a few minutes.

She started to twitch as her blood sugar dropped. I removed the two suitcases and hauled her to the top of the stairs. It reminded me of my mother's death. Then I pushed her down. She clattered down and came to rest awkwardly at the bottom. But she hadn't really done any damage to herself. So I gripped her head and rammed it as hard as I could into the bottom step. I repeated it and the skin burst open and the wound started to bleed. That should do it. I peeled off the tape from her face and went back upstairs.

I left an empty box of 10mg Diazepam by her bed with half a glass of water and retrieved the Gladstone bag.

I tidied up the Indian takeaway and put the tracksuit bottoms at the top of the stairs as if the woman had tripped over them. I looked around. It should be convincing enough.

I went back into the kitchen, repaired the lock on the back door as best as I could and left.

I didn't hear anything for a couple of weeks, then the RSPCA inspector bought in a stray cat.

'You remember Shadow and Cody?'

I nodded.

'Well, you don't need to write the statement and won't need to go to court. The woman had an accident and fell down the stairs at her house and had a brain haemorrhage. It was days before the police found her. The neighbours complained of a foul smell. They think she took an overdose of diazepam.'

'How's Cody?' I asked.

'Doing really well, she put on weight in the kennels and has gone to a good home in Chelmsford.'

Dingo

Mr Tibbles had made himself at home and decided his day bed would be on my desk looking out of the window onto the small garden where he could watch the wildlife. I don't think he ever caught anything, he was too well fed.

The sailing continued throughout the summer but my doctor friend was becoming more and more morose. Eventually, he confided in me that his wife was having an affair with the pro at the local tennis club. They were getting divorced and he was moving up to London to one of the teaching hospitals. He offered me his boat at a really good price and I had no hesitation in buying it. I could easily manage to sail it on my own.

A few days after I completed the sale of the boat, a big, shaven-head man brought into the clinic a young staffie called Dingo. It was late one Friday evening. Dingo had multiple dog-fight wounds all over his body that looked a few days old and were already infected. The man was very agitated and asked if I could stitch his dog up that evening with soluble sutures.

Dingo was absolutely terrified. But I sedated him, cleaned the wounds and sutured them as best I could. I gave Dingo a long acting antibiotic injection and a pain killer and warned the owner that Dingo would be sleepy for the next couple of hours. But he didn't appear to listen. Whatever or who ever had done this to the dog had petrified it. There was a mixture of pain and pleading in his eyes, begging me not to let the man take him home. But, as I had no proof, there was nothing legally I could do. I could contact the RSPCA but whether they could do anything without firm evidence I doubted it. The police wouldn't be interested. He was my last patient and curiosity got the better of me so I followed the man in his van. It was easy because it had a giant uPVC window on side.

Eventually, we got to an industrial estate in Basildon and he parked his van outside an old garage. There were lots of other cars parked there so I parked my car outside some offices, put some drugs and a syringe into my pockets in case I would need them and walked cautiously down to the garage. I looked through a broken side window into the garage. I could see some men standing around a pit that was lit with spot lights whilst the rest was in darkness. There was a metal staircase going up to mezzanine floor and a small office. In the darkness, I climbed up and watched from there.

The man I had followed stood above the pit with Dingo. The dog's tail was between his legs and he was shaking. He was still suffering the effects of the sedative. I wished I had been more decisive and not given the man the dog back. Bets were being called out but no-one wanted to bet on the staffie. On the other side was a thin man with dirty blonde hair and a wispy beard. He was taunting the bald man. He had a huge black and tan dog that looked like a Rottweiler/Mastiff cross.

'You not up for it, Dean. Can't put your dog where your mouth is. You're just scared, are you? Tell you what. Give me a couple of grand and you can go.' The thin man laughed.

Dean hesitated then pushed Dingo into the pit. I could see the dog didn't want to go in and struggled to stay out of the pit but he lost his footing and tumbled in, landing on his back. The thin man unleashed his dog.

The dog jumped into the pit on its own. It knew what to do.

The giant black and tan dog lunged at Dingo, who just cowered in terror. The giant dog tossed the staffie in the air and caught it in its giant jaws, ripping at its throat. The staffie whimpered and the black and tan dog tossed it into a corner to die.

The thin man laughed.

'Don't think you'll get that repaired this time, Dean. He's a goner and you need to finish him off.' The thin man handed Dean a hammer. Dean took it, unsure of what to do, then raised the hammer above Dingo's head. The first blow bounced off the dog's thick skull. The thin man laughed.

'What do you go to the gym for, Dean? Is that the best you can do? My mother could do better than that.' The others in the crowd laughed.

Dean rolled up his sleeves, swung the hammer over his head and bought it down on the dog's head as if he was doing a strength fairground ride. The hammer sank into dog's skull, splattering bone, brains and blood over Dean who picked up his dog and tossed it into a skip in a dark corner. He picked up a rag and wiped his hands.

Dean went back to the pit where the next fight was about to take place and bets were being taken. The huge black and tan dog was taking on all comers.

I slipped down the stairs and looked at Dingo. He was covered in jagged wounds where the other dog had bitten it.

They were deep and the skin had been ripped away from the underlying flesh. Folds of skin hung limply from the wounds. His head was a mess. The skull had been cracked open like an egg. There was little blood but brains, skin and hair were smeared all around the wound. I found it hard to look at it. Just as I turned away, I saw the dog's chest move. It still seemed alive; how I didn't know. There was obviously no hope for him so I injected some pentobarbitone into his heart with long needle. Dingo gave a small sigh as he died. Then I was sick.

I felt the rage rise within me; this man didn't deserve to live after what he had done to that poor dog.

I followed him home. I was tempted to do something there and then but that would be rash. It needed planning so I started watching him.

For two weeks, I watched and followed Dean. It looked like he lived with his son. He was an uPVC window fitter. During the week, he would leave home at 8.00 and drive to the factory where he would pick up the windows he was fitting that day. He would work until 4.00pm then he would meet his son at the gym where he would train for just over an hour. He would get changed in the changing room where he would drink half of a protein drink he bought with him. Then he would lock up his bag and drink in one of the lockers.

After training, he would get out his bag and drink from the locker and lay it untidily on the bench then he would have a shower for at least 10 minutes before sitting down on the bench to drink the rest of his drink and talk to his son. He would casually get dressed then pick up his bag, put the empty drink container inside and leave and drive home in his van.

The protein drink was the way to do it. I mixed up a solution of phenobarbitone, Lanoxin and immobilon. The immobilon was liquid but the other two were in tablet form. I crushed several tablets of each separately and mixed each with water in a 5 ml syringe periodically shaking them. After a couple of hours, I carefully decanted the fluid and discarded the remnants of the tablet. I mixed the two liquids together and added some immobilon and injected it into a 20ml phial. That should be more than enough. It did taste a bit bitter but the protein drink should disguise the taste.

The next day, I followed Dean into the health club and waited for an hour in the car, reading a book. Then I picked up a sailing bag I used for my waterproofs and went into the health centre. I paid cash and told the receptionist I was meeting someone to play squash.

I sat in a dark corner of the changing room and waited for Dean to come in. He came in panting and sweating. He opened his locker, pulled out the bag and drinks and took a long swig. I was worried he would drink all of it but he put the container down, took off his sweaty clothes and headed for the showers.

I waited a minute then went over to his bag. I picked up the drink container and was about to unscrew it when someone came in.

I took the container over to my dark corner, unscrewed the lid and injected my potion. The person who had come in went to the toilets so I put the drink back in Dean's bag and left.

After half an hour, I heard the ambulance come screaming into the carpark. Two green-liveried paramedics jumped out, took a stretcher from the back of the ambulance and rushed into the health centre.

After a little while, they reappeared, wheeling Dean. At least, I assumed it was Dean. I couldn't see who it was; they were covered in blankets and medical equipment.

After Dean's death, I started trying to formulate drug cocktails that were tasteless yet potent. I wanted to try and avoid using the immobilon unless I had to.

My particular favourite was a mixture of Tramadol, diazepam and phenobarbitone. There was always a plentiful supply of these from people returning drugs whose pets had died. I made this up in a 50ml phial that I kept in the fridge.

I realised that if I continued to use Immobilon, an experienced post-mortem and modern toxicology would soon arouse suspicions. I needed to be very careful.

Up to now, the 'deaths' could be explained as accidents or overdoses but sooner or later, someone was sure to suspect. I started getting paranoid. Imagining I was being watched; I started sleeping badly.

Mad Dog

A giant headless dog, its skin hanging off its body like a cloak, was chasing me around the deserted garage trying to swallow me in the black void that was its head. It howled loudly and continuously. I couldn't escape; it blocked all the doors I tried. The garage was dark with an eerie red glow coming through the ceiling.

I awoke in a sweat, shaking uncontrollably. The dog in the skip haunted me during the day and every night, despite how much I drank. I had never seen anything like it. Even the worst RTA was nothing compared to it. I felt sick thinking about it. I had no dreams, just nightmares. The dog's smashed head demanded revenge. I knew the only way to get peace was to kill the thin man.

I became obsessed with finding him. Nothing else mattered. Most nights I would drive past the dog-fight garage but it remained deserted. My bridge was erratic and disjointed. I started drinking heavily so I couldn't concentrate and my bidding was irrational and my card-playing inept. The invitations to play quickly dried up.

At work, I was short with the clients and unfairly critical of the staff, who actively avoided me. In the end, I became the designated charity vet and liaised with the inspectors who didn't seem to mind my irritability and the clients who couldn't afford normal treatment were grateful for any help. It was one of the inspectors who shook me out of my dark mood. He was an ex-policeman and took me out for a drink and demanded an explanation. At first, I was reluctant to speak. But after a couple of beers, I told him an edited version about the staffie with the bite wounds. I told him I had put it to sleep but not the exact circumstances. When I described the thin man, he nodded.

'That's Dave House. His nickname is Mad Dog. He lives somewhere on Canvey Island, I think. Although he moves around quite a lot.' The inspector looked at me, rubbed his head as if thinking then continued, 'I came across him when I was with Essex Police. He's a nasty piece of work. He's involved in most criminal activity in South East Essex. Drugs, smuggling cigarettes, car theft, copper wire theft, lead from roofs—that sort of thing. He's not someone you want to cross. He's called Mad Dog because he bit someone in a prison fight; the wound became so badly infected that the man nearly died. The name stuck because he seemed to like it but no-one calls him that to his face.'

The inspector sipped his beer.

'There are rumours of another dog-fight coming up, possibly with dogs from outside the area. If I get the details, I'll let you know. But we can't tackle him without police. It would be too dangerous. If I hear anything, don't worry, I'll let you know.'

The inspector gave me some hope so at weekends, I took the boat out. It helped me clean my mind. I would have to wait for the RSPCA inspector to get back to me. I started taking Mr Tibbles onto the boat for company. He enjoyed being on deck watching the world go by. He had his favourite spot just in front of the cabin hatch where I would put a towel and he would nap with one eye open watching the seagulls. I had seen several dogs with life jackets but Mr Tibbles wasn't having it. Despite his weight, he was very nimble and weaved his way in between the sails and sheets with ease.

The inspector came to see me at the end of evening surgery one Friday night. He came with a policeman instead of a pet. It was the same policeman who had been involved with Shadow and Cody. We nodded in recognition to one another.

'It's tonight. On Canvey island; in a warehouse near the oil refinery. It's a big meeting. There are supposed to be some dogs coming up from South West London. You can follow us in your car if you like. Just stay out the way, but bring your medicine bag; we may need your professional skills.'

I followed the car onto the island and headed towards the lit-up refinery. Cars turned off towards the houses until there were just the headlights of our two cars. We pulled into an old petrol station. The inspector got out and ambled across to my car.

'It's just after nine o'clock. We'll wait here for an hour or so to let them get set up and then move in. There are a couple more patrol cars coming the other way from Basildon. We'll meet them at the warehouse.'

He went back to his car and I turned on the radio. It was Classic FM. Just the sort of soothing music I needed. I was vaguely aware of cars and vans speeding past with no headlights on as I drifted off to sleep.

The headless dog was chasing me. I could feel its breath behind me. I tried to run faster but no matter how fast I ran it was catching me up. Where its head should have been became a mass of teeth dribbling with blood. Its body was dark with no real form. It was nearly upon me. I tied to speed up but it was upon me. I was about to disappear into the grinding teeth when the tapping at my window woke me up, sweating and shaking. I wound down the window.

'You OK?' The inspector asked.

I nodded.

'Good. It's time to move off. Follow us but don't use your headlights.'

I looked at my watch. It was just after 11.00pm.

We drove slowly for about a mile then came to a warehouse. There were shards of light piercing through the windows that had thick drapes on the inside.

I followed the policeman and inspector to the other side of the building. There were two other policemen waiting by a window they had prised open. The two men nodded and we all entered the building through the window.

We were in a storeroom that had a few dusty car parts stacked on the shelves.

Through the half-open door, we could see that there were about twenty-five people in the warehouse. More than had been at the last fight. They all men except for a plump, grey-haired woman with a stall at the back. She had a small table lit by a lantern, piled high with bottles and boxes, syringes and needles. She was doing a roaring trade. From what I could see, there were boxes of antibiotics, anti-inflammatories, anti-septic solutions and disposable suture kits. I thought I had seen her before at the practice. I didn't think she was a vet so goodness knew where they had come from.

In the half light, I could see various dogs being led around. The majority had some Pit Bull in them. But there were two massive great mastiffs, probably the biggest dogs I had ever seen. They were being led by a huge coloured man. All muscle bulging out of his clothes. Not a man to cross. His dogs had thick studded leather collars and were being led with thick metal chains. A lot of the dogs had badly docked tails whose stunted ends were swollen and gnarled. Many had mutilated ears whose jagged edges pointed upwards in deformed defiance. These had not been done by a vet. All the dogs were covered in scars and a couple were salivating in anticipation.

Bales of straw were being arranged in a rough square like a boxing ring. The "arena" was lit on three sides by the cab mounted spotlights of 4x4's. There was a gap in the middle of the fourth side. Behind were two much smaller pens made of metal railings. I could see "Mad Dog" standing on a bale of straw organising the others. Next to him on another bale was a large fat man in a faded dark suit, sorting out wads of notes. He was the bookie. When the lights were switched on, the rest of the warehouse was dark and shadowy. There were muffled sounds of talk and dogs on chains. The occasional cigarette being lit highlighted a face for a second.

A young shaven-head man struggled into the ring with a crate containing two whimpering dogs crammed inside. They looked well fed so were probably people's pets that had been stolen. Both had wet and soiled themselves in fear.

They were tipped out of the crate and pushed into the ring. One was a young female golden Labrador, barely a year old. She had a collar and tag on her neck. A loved family pet that had been stolen for tonight. The other was a male black and white border collie, a little older, but not castrated. They cowered in a corner, hugging each other in terror. The border collie tried to escape through the straw bales but was hit with a stick and forced back in with a muted howl.

'Right!' Shouted Mad Dog. 'Let's have some fun.'

There was a hush in the room. I could see movement from the back and hear some dogs pulling on their chains.

The two dogs were led into the ring by their handler, a big ginger-haired man with a red face and piggy little eyes. He was laughing. They were huge Rottweiler crosses pulling hard on their chains.

'Right, Mick. Welcome to Essex. Let's see what the dogs from Bermondsey can do,' goaded Mad Dog.

The ginger man was cheered by half a dozen men standing in a group. He smiled at them then bent down nervously to unleash his dogs. I could see he was afraid and the dogs sensed this. One snarled at him and he quickly slipped the chains before hastily retreating behind the bales of straw.

The two dogs sniffed and raised their heads; they could smell the two dogs cowering in the corner. They looked at each other and bounded over the ring. The Labrador rolled over on her back submissively as if hoping to appease the two snarling dogs but they just tore into her, ripping her to pieces. Steam rose from their mouths and nostrils and blood dripped from their mouths as they tossed away the remains of the Labrador.

The border collie made one last attempt to escape before it was dragged back into the ring by a back leg. It turned and bared its teeth at the two dogs. It made a brave attempt to defend itself before suffering the same fate.

There was laughter from the crowd.

It reminded me when my mother had taken me to see the local hunt and we had witnessed the pack of hounds tearing apart a fox.

I turned and threw up in the corner behind me. The policeman and inspector looked horrified at what they had seen. The ginger-headed man was laughing. I wanted to stop this now but they held me back.

'The others will be here soon. Then we will get the lot of them,' the policeman whispered.

'Are you ready for a real fight?' Mad Dog announced. 'I've got something special for you tonight. Two dogs from Essex against two dogs from Bermondsey.'

I could see the mastiffs being brought closer to the ring. The ginger-haired man stopped laughing. The penny had dropped. His dogs wouldn't be quite so hungry for a fight.

The two mastiffs were led into the ring to loud roars from the crowd. Their huge heads with docked ears made them look very frightening. The rottweilers turned to look at them. Their stumpy tails dropped. The mastiffs licked their lips, looked at each other and launched themselves at the two rottweilers. But the black dogs were waiting and sidestepped the mastiffs and bit deep on the back legs.

There were growls and squeals accompanied by roars from the crowd but I couldn't watch and turned away. I could just make out a siren in the background. Then another and then a third. No-one else seemed to have heard anything. The noise of the dog-fight and the cheering of the spectators drowned everything else out. But I saw Mad Dog shrink into the shadows, taking his dog with him. I nudged the policeman, he nodded and we circled around the warehouse to try and cut

Mad Dog off. I opened my Gladstone bag and loaded up a syringe with a powerful sedative. Just in case.

The sirens were more obvious now and the crowd was starting to disperse. We hurried out of the warehouse and saw Mad Dog by a van.

'Stop!' shouted the policeman.

I saw something black hurtle towards the policeman. It was Mad Dog's dog. The policeman froze in fear as the dog lunged at his arm. I grabbed it by the tail with one hand and injected it with the other. It let go of the policeman and turned towards me. But I had had enough experience of lunging dogs and I moved out of the way. The policeman recovered himself as the dog collapsed.

The policeman rubbed his arm, blood was dripping freely from it.

'Kill it!' He shouted to me. 'Kill it.'

I shouldn't have, I know. But I knew that a court would agree as it had attacked a policeman. I looked down at the dog; he was peacefully asleep. His teeth were jagged and chipped. His body was covered with ugly scars that were proud and uneven crossed with thick bars where the bite wounds had been poorly sutured. He was the victim of his master. I stroked his head softly, he wouldn't feel anything. Surely this was better that being kept in a cage until a sentence was agreed and passed. I filled up a syringe with pentobarbitone and gently injected it into the dog's heart. After a few seconds, he let out a couple of deep breaths and was gone.

'I'll take him back to the practice and arrange his cremation.'

'I owe you one, Doc. That dog would have killed me.'

The police arrived in several vans. Most of the men were arrested and their dogs taken away. We managed to get the mastiffs and rottweilers into different vans. They weren't re-homeable so would probably be euthanised.

The woman with the drugs and Mad Dog were the only two who managed to get away.

The RSPCA inspector collected the remains of the two dogs and their collars.

'I'll try and come up with some story. At least, they will know that they are dead; but not how.'

I took Mad Dog's dog back to the practice and put it in the freezer ready for cremation. I went upstairs to the staffroom, made a cup of tea and sat down on the sofa.

It was the smell of fresh coffee that awoke me. Two nurses on the early shift had put on the coffee machine and were wondering what to do with me.

'What time is it?' I asked yawning.

'It's quarter to eight,' came a giggled reply.

'What day is it?'

'It's Saturday. I don't think you are on call.'

I scratched my head and felt my unshaven face.

'What's the weather like?'

'There's a bit of a breeze, but it's sunny, not a cloud in the sky. Do you want some coffee?'

I nodded and was given a hot cup. Once the caffeine started working, I got up and looked out of the window. It was a perfect day for sailing. I looked at the tide times in the booklet in my pocket. High tide was in an hour. I would go home, grab Mr Tibbles and we would take the boat out. The shower and shave would have to wait.

I drove home and quickly got Mr Tibbles and some water and food for lunch then set off for the marina. What I failed to notice was a thin bearded man with dirty blond hair on a motorbike at the end of the road. I just wanted to get to the marina. I don't think I looked once in the rear-view mirror.

I took Mr Tibbles in one hand and the lunch things in the other and walked down to the berth. I let Mr Tibbles out and he settled down on an old blanket by the mast. I undid the ropes at bow then I went down below and stowed lunch away. I thought I heard something up above, but when I got back on deck, I could see nothing unusual. I started the engine and slipped the two ropes on either side in the stern. It was exactly high tide and the boat eased out of the berth and I turned to follow the tide as it went out into the sun. There wasn't much in front of me so I set the course, switched on the automatic pilot and went around the boat pulling in the fenders.

I finished in the bow and turned. There was Mad Dog by the wheel, brandishing a knife. He must have gone down into the cabin whilst I was at the bow.

'I thought I recognised you. You killed my dog, now I'm going to kill you. Then I'll cut you up and feed you to the fishes. No-one will ever know.'

I felt the hate well up inside me. I looked around for a weapon. There was nothing to hand then I remembered that there were the two winch handles hanging by the mast if I could get to them.

Mad Dog flicked the knife from one hand to the other; he knew what he was doing. He moved purposely towards me.

'Are you ready to die? Slowly. I'm going to kill you. Then I'm going to sink your boat and your cat where no-one can find you.' He laughed, squinting into the sun. He tried to move on the deck to get out of the sun. But there was nothing to provide any shadow. Then he lunged at me around the mast then the knife switched hands and he lunged the other side of the mast, catching my sailing jacket. He edged forwards, waving the knife and trying to force me back. He was trying to get to the other side of the mast. If he did that, I had no chance.

Suddenly, there was a shadow on Mad Dog's face and something landed on it. It was Mr Tibbles, all his claws sticking into Mad Dog's face. Mad Dog screamed and dropped the knife. I rushed forward, grabbed a winch handle as Mr Tibbles disappeared down the hatchway. I smashed it into Mad Dog's face as hard as I could, he staggered a little and I kept on hitting him. He fell on the deck but I didn't stop. I just kept on hitting him.

A huge shadow loomed in front on me. It was a barge going upriver. I hurriedly switched off the automatic pilot, swerved the boat out of the way and killed the engine.

I knelt down in the stern. Mad Dog was hardly breathing. His face was unrecognisable. I went down to the cabin and got some pentobarbitone from the Gladstone bag. When I got back on deck, Mr Tibbles was back on his perch by the mast. I injected Mad Dog and he ebbed away.

Mr Tibbles looked down at me from his perch by the mast, meowed and licked his lips. He was hungry. I shrugged my shoulders and went down to the galley to find him some food.

When I got back on deck, I looked at the body. What was I going to do with it? I could go back to the marina and tell the police. But that didn't appeal. Or I could do what Mad Dog was going to do and dump it in the sea. I started looking through the lockers and found the spare sails. I could wrap him up in a piece of sail. I went forward to the anchor locker. There was so much chain.

There were some bolt cutters downstairs.

I managed to cut off a piece of chain which I wrapped around Mad Dog's body then roughly cut a piece of sail and wrapped him up in it. At least, I didn't have to look at him anymore.

I motored the boat out to sea until the sea bottom was a long way down. I stopped the boat and dragged Mad Dog's body over the side. It disappeared quickly in a few ripples.

I put the sails up and we sailed leisurely for two hours up the coast. Mr Tibbles sat by the mast, staring into the horizon. I found on the chart plotter a suitable sheltered anchorage and I headed towards it.

I dropped anchor and Mr Tibbles and I spent a peaceful evening under the stars with a cooling westerly breeze. I found some sausages and mash which we shared and some whisky that we didn't.

It was the best sleep I had had for ages. No nightmares, just deep refreshing sleep. In fact, I had no more nightmares after that. Well, apart from one.

Why Mr Tibbles went for Mad Dog I'll never know. Maybe he took exception to his comments but he saved my life.

Not All Bad

After Mad Dog's death, life settled into a routine that quickly became a little boring. I found myself feeling negative and unfulfilled. I worked part-time at the practice and spent the rest of the time sailing or reading. I even managed the odd game of bridge and managed to win most of the rubbers I played.

Mr Tibbles and I had an established routine. He would wake me up in the morning by jumping up onto my bed and purring loudly into my ear. I would get up and shower then make coffee and feed him. I would go to work via the café leaving him asleep on his armchair in the lounge or on my desk. If I was working, he would greet me on my return when I would feed him and in the evening, we would each have our own armchairs until he decided it was bedtime when he would jump onto my lap and kneed me until I got up and we went to bed. I slept on the right and he slept on the left.

He had a cat flap so he could go into the garden but he always seemed hesitant to use it and would prefer that I opened the door for him. He would stand patiently at the door, looking up at me expectantly.

Summer clouded into autumn with rain and shorter days and the boat was taken out of the water for winter. I had plenty of money but I found myself watching too much television and drinking too much in the evening. I needed stimulating.

One day a young couple brought in a cross collie female called Bella to see me. I could smell the dog in the waiting room. Bella was an unspayed bitch in a terrible condition: matted and dirty with a huge mammary tumour that had ulcerated and was dripping blood everywhere. The poor dog had the fetid stench of infection and necrosis.

There was something about the couple I didn't like. He was a scrawny, dark, southern European type who insisted on wearing a baseball cap, the wrong way round, on top of thick black hair. There was something familiar about him. He was unshaven and wore dark glasses in the consulting room. He wore jeans torn at the knee and a hooded top. I could see he was wearing a smart-looking watch, possibly an Omega, but he pulled down the sleeve when he saw me looking at it. He hardly spoke, but when he did, I could see his teeth were stained with nicotine. He obviously had no interest in the dog, or the dog in him.

Bella was a sweet-natured bitch who allowed me to examine her. I could see the pain and distress in her eyes. She had tried to clean the tumour and saliva mixed with blood dripped from her mouth. The dog either needed surgery or euthanasia but the couple was reluctant to do anything. Normally, I was sympathetic to owners who had little money but there was something about this couple; I didn't trust them.

'She was my mum's dog. Aren't there any tablets you can give?' The girl asked. She looked dirty in a faded blue dress. Her long dark brown hair was unwashed and un-brushed.

'Bella needs a big operation to remove the tumour, otherwise it would be kinder for her to be put to sleep. It's unfair on her to leave her like this. I'll give her a pain killing injection and an antibiotic. That will help tonight. Have a think about it then come back and see me tomorrow,' I replied.

They didn't come back the next day but I did see an elderly man shuffling with a walking stick with an equally elderly golden retriever called Dexter. They hobbled in unison into my consulting room. Both were obviously in pain and the retriever had several warts that were discharging and appalling teeth that needed an anaesthetic and a dental. The dog clearly meant the world to the man and the man to the dog.

He had thin grey hair and stubble but a kind face. His clothes were worn and threadbare and he had a white band on his wrist where a watch had been.

When I quoted him, blood drained from his face and he steadied himself on my consulting room table.

'Let me see what I can do,' he said and looked down at his dog. 'If it has to be done then I may be able to find some more money. I can't let him suffer.'

I wished I could help him. But there was no national health for pets.

That evening, I decided to go and see the couple with the collie cross. I didn't have anything else to do and Mr Tibbles was asleep in his armchair.

I took my potion out of the fridge and put it the Gladstone bag.

The couple lived in an old house down an unmade road just out of town. It was on its own surrounded by fields and woodland. There was no-one else about, just a black 4x4, possibly a RAV4, that arrived just after me and parked on the other side of the road. I left my car a little way away, picked up my Gladstone bag instinctively and walked to the house.

There was an old transit van parked outside but when I looked through the garage doors, I could see that there was a brand new BMW. The penny dropped. I had seen that car once before when I had dealt with the yob and Billy, the staffie.

There was an old stable were Bella was loosely tied up. There was no bedding, and empty water and food bowls. It was shameful neglect. The dog stirred from her sleep and looked up at me and wagged her tail. I filled up her water bowl from an outside tap. I had a few dog treats in my pocket and gave them to her which she wolfed down and looked up for more. Sadly, there were none so she had a long drink, put her head back on her front paws and went to sleep.

There was a light on in the kitchen and the rest of the house was in darkness. As I walked up to it, I could see the girl at a table listening to music and smoking a joint. At the back of the room, there was a slightly opened door through which shone bright light. But the windows were heavily draped to prevent any light from escaping. It seemed to be full of green plants. The kitchen door was unlocked. I could see a wad of notes on the table and plastic bags full of dried leaves. I felt the anger build up; the dog deserved better.

The man came into the room carrying bunches of leaves that he placed on a sideboard. He still wore his cap and shades. I could understand the shades as the light from the plant room was intensely bright. He picked up some of the plastic bags which he put in a small holdall. He said something to the girl then picked up some keys from the table.

I hid around the side of the house as he came out, opened the garage and roared off in the BMW.

I looked through the window again, the girl was still listening to music through headphones and the joint was nearly finished. There were the remains of a pizza on the table beside her and half a glass of Coke. She got up and went to the bathroom. I loaded 10mls of my potion into a syringe and carefully went into the kitchen. I emptied it into her drink then hurried out. She came back in, put on her headphones and slurped the rest of her drink.

After 10 minutes, she slumped in the chair. I removed the headphones and could hear some strange music. I loaded a syringe with morphine and injected it into her. That would make for interesting toxicology. I looked at her then thought of the poor dog in the stable. I put my hand over her mouth and pinched her nose so she couldn't breathe. Even with all the drugs in her body, instinct made her fight for air but to no avail. After a couple of minutes, she was dead. I put the headphones back on and positioned her body so she looked asleep.

The wad of notes on the table amounted to £1500. It was much more than was needed to pay for the dog's operation and aftercare.

I looked around the kitchen, there wasn't much in it. There were the remains of countless takeaway meals slung in a corner beside a heaped bin buzzing with flies.

I went through the door to the plant room. It was a converted lounge/dining room. There must have been thirty marijuana plants in large pots under bright lights with rubber tubes feeding them with water.

At the end of the room was a table where leaves were being dried.

I wasn't sure what to do now. It made sense to wait for the man. Dispatch him and then torch the place. I would take Bella back with me and operate on her tomorrow.

So I waited.

I had seen a wooden pickaxe handle outside the dog's stable. I took the remains of the pizza to feed the dog, which she demolished, retrieved the pickaxe handle and waited beside the kitchen door.

In about half an hour, I heard the BWM return. The man came into the kitchen and as he started to speak to the girl, I hit him as hard as I could on the baseball cap on his head. He crumpled to the floor. The baseball cap flew off but amazingly, his dark glasses stayed on. I gave him a large dose of morphine and pressed the syringe into his hand.

I put my hand over his mouth and nose. His hands waved a little in protest but then he was still. I looked at the watch on his wrist. It was an Omega Speedmaster. Well, he wouldn't need it and I knew someone who did so I put it in my pocket. I checked his pockets; there was another £500 which I took.

The girl's joint was half finished and had gone out. I re-lit it and tore up some of the cardboard wrapping and placed it beside the girl's chair. There was an old newspaper and I added a couple of pages then tossed the lit joint on top. At first, nothing happened, so I blew on the joint and a few sparks came out. I blew again and the newspaper ignited. I added some more newspaper and then the fire started to take hold.

I looked at the scene from the kitchen door. The syringe was in the man's hand and it looked like the girl had dropped the joint.

It looked like a tragic accident. The fire was really taking hold so I shut the door and went to the stable.

Bella was happy to go with me and as we drove down the track, I could see a dull glow in my rear view mirror.

There were no cars about, just the RAV4 I had seen earlier. I drove the dog back to the hospital and handed her over to the nurse as a stray I would sort out later. We put her on a drip, cleaned her as best we could and put a big sign on the cage saying 'nil by mouth op tomorrow.'

I was up early the next day and walked around to Dexter's house. His owner was surprised to see me but asked me in and made me a cup of tea. The house was like the owner—threadbare. The carpets were worn and the curtains thin. But the house was spotlessly clean. There were no pictures on the walls, just hooks where they had been. On the kitchen table were some cufflinks and an old cigarette case.

The man looked at them embarrassingly but I smiled at him.

'I've some good news for Dexter. I wanted to tell you straight away. A client has just given me some money on the strict instruction that no-one must know who they are.'

'He has given me some money to help specific patients that I think are deserving, so I thought of Dexter.' I pulled the money out of my pocket. 'Here is £1,000. This is for Dexter's operation and dental and aftercare. It should be more than enough. You can use the rest to make sure he has some decent food.'

The man looked at me, unsure of what to do.

'No-one will know but you and me. That's the donor's wishes.' I reached into my pocket. 'Just one more thing.' I took out the watch and handed it to him. 'This is for Dexter. Should he need any help in the future, you can use it. In the meantime, I suggest you wear it for safekeeping.'

I handed the man the watch and left.

The rest of the money paid for Bella's operation which I did later on that day; I removed the tumour and spayed her then contacted the local re-homing centre. I am glad to say Bella had a new home within a week. They changed her name to Lady.

One of the other vets operated on Dexter; dentals were not my favourite procedure. I saw Dexter and his owner in the waiting room for a post-op check. Dexter looked fantastic and the owner was wearing the watch.

The local news reported the fire as a tragic accident. It hardly mentioned the cannabis plants.

Possy

It was raining outside. I peered through the bedroom curtains. It was cold, wet and miserable; a typical March day. I had trudged through winter, hid myself away at Christmas and developed a taste for malt whiskey donated by clients through January and February. I barely saw anyone outside the practice. In fact, apart from the supermarket, I didn't see anyone. It might nearly be spring but it felt like it was still mid-winter.

I didn't want to get up, let alone go to work. I felt empty and motiveless. It felt as if there was a huge weight pressing down on me and I just wanted to stay in bed. My mind felt dark and black. I had no family to speak of. My father didn't count. I wasn't in any meaningful relationship, a few had tried but I still mourned Meg. I caught myself looking at the Gladstone bag. I knew that there would be something in there that would help.

Mr Tibbles jumped onto the bed and meowed. It was time for his breakfast.

I knew the signs of depression. Most of my colleagues had suffered, it's just I thought I would be stronger. I needed a break; I suspect Mad Dog was still in my head.

I had no-one to look after Mr Tibbles and I didn't want to put him in a cattery. We would have to travel together. We could take the boat but I really wanted to go further afield—a bit of sun and adventure.

I turned on the TV and went into the kitchen to feed Mr Tibbles and make some coffee. I came back into the lounge and sat down in the armchair. I looked at the TV but nothing registered then my brain engaged. There was a competition for a motor home. That was it; a boat on wheels. Mr Tibbles and I could go to France and maybe northern Spain. We could take two or three months off. Perfect.

I felt as if I had some purpose now. I finished my coffee, had a quick shower and went to work.

When I explained the situation to my boss, he was full of sympathy and agreed as soon as I was ready to go, I could. If I wanted a job when I came back, that wouldn't be a problem. I didn't care; I had enough money anyway. We agreed I could leave at the end of the week. Already, I felt my spirits lifting.

On my last day, as I said goodbye to the receptionists, I notice a black Toyota RAV4 in the car park. A bald, stout middle-aged man with a thin moustache got out, looked at me quizzically then went into the reception. I was puzzled I thought it was the same car that I had seen at the drug farm. I drove around the block and when the car had left, I went back into the practice.

'Oh he was just asking a few questions about you, said he was buying a new puppy and had been recommended to use you as his vet.'

'Did he make an appointment?' I asked.

'No. Said he would think about it.'

I thought no more about it; that weekend, I found a second-hand Possl Summit for sale in Oxfordshire. I took the train up there in case I could drive it back!

Alas no; I put down a deposit, transferred the money during the week and drove it back the following weekend.

Mr Tibbles' pet passport was in order and so we loaded up Possy, as I called the motor home, and set off for Folkestone. At the terminal, I bought some food and was persuaded to buy some yellow-lensed night driving that I was assured would help me against the glaring lights of oncoming traffic at night.

The journey from Calais was unexciting. It was raining and the land was flat and wet but we kept going southwest with one night here and two nights there. Both Mr Tibbles and I developed quite a taste for seafood and I for wine. We headed for La Rochelle and from there to Bordeaux.

Over six weeks, I became a different man. I put on weight and started to tan. I hardly recognised myself in the mirror. My French had progressed beyond "Bonjour" and "Merci" and my palate enjoyed exploring the different markets. I never knew that there were so many different cheeses. I started buying wine to take back to the UK and realised that I needed more fridge storage space if the wine was to stay at its best so I found a garage on the way to Arcachon who fitted a customised top-loading fridge under the bed.

'You could get a body in that.' The mechanic had laughed.

I had no idea that motor homes were so popular and so versatile.

We continued past the Dune de Pilat and headed south through the Landes forest down to Hossegor where I had several unsuccessful attempts at surfing, Capbreton and finally Biarritz. When I stood at the Rocher de la Vierge, I could see Spain across the sea.

By this time, I was longing for a bigger, softer bed; maybe when they put the fridge in, they did something to the bed. I wasn't that far down the motorway from San Sebastian. So we drove straight there; I checked into a terrace suite on the top floor at the Maria Cristina hotel. It wasn't cheap but I felt I could just about afford it and besides, we deserved it. Unfortunately, the motor home wouldn't fit into the underground carpark so I unloaded what I needed, much to the amusement of the bereted doorman, installed Mr Tibbles and the luggage in the room, and drove Possy to the "camping car" carpark and got a taxi back.

The room was on the fifth floor with a terrace overlooking the river. There was a large sitting room and an equally large bedroom with an enormous bed. I got a small duvet from housekeeping for Mr Tibbles, I left the sitting room door to the terrace ajar, put the litter tray on the terrace and left him sleeping whilst I explored the town.

The next few days, I enjoyed all the hospitality of San Sebastian. I even sent a postcard to my old practice. Every morning, Mr Tibbles and I would eat breakfast on the terrace. I would sample different delights from the enormous buffet and Mr Tibbles enjoyed smoked salmon and a variety of cheeses. Each morning, the restaurant manager came over to talk. I am sure he just wanted to improve his English, which was very good. I told him I was a vet and my wife had recently died. I also told him an edited version of how I acquired Mr Tibbles. It seemed easier to talk to strangers.

One evening outside my room, I noticed a commotion along the corridor; apparently, one of the hotel guests had been taken ill. I thought no more about it until breakfast when the manager came over with an elegant woman possibly in her fifties.

'Good morning.' The manager drew up an extra chair and asked the lady to sit down. 'This is Mrs Rossini, she has a slight problem and I thought you could help. This is the English veterinary surgeon I was telling you about.' He smiled at me and hovered in the background.

The lady held out her hand; we shook hands, barely touching.

'Eleanor Rossini.' She had a strong assertive voice. But I couldn't place the accent.

She must have seen the puzzled look on my face and laughed. 'I'm Canadian. We're nicer than Americans.'

'Would you like some coffee?' I asked politely, not sure if I wanted this intrusion into my breakfast. Mr Tibbles looked at her then curled up on his chair.

'Thank you.' The manager summoned a waitress who was dispatched for the coffee and disappeared.

I had seen her and her companion at the breakfast buffet. I remember she had commented how delicious one of the cakes I had been helping myself to looked.

It turned out it was her companion who had been taken ill. Nothing serious, just a 24-hour bug. Mrs Rossini had organised a tour to Bilbao but was reluctant to go on her own so the manager had suggested me.

Normally, I would have politely declined but I must have been in a good mood; besides, I hadn't anything else to do so I agreed. I put Mr Tibbles in the room and went back downstairs. There was a large black Mercedes waiting and the two of us got in the back.

We made polite conversation on the way there and seemed to warm to each other as the journey progressed. We were dropped off by the Guggenheim Museum in Bilbao. I found the building itself fascinating and the giant puppy and spider on the outside more interesting than the exhibits inside. Then we went for a late lunch. The Spanish, unlike the French, are happy to eat late. We went to a smart restaurant and had a selection of pintxos which were very good. I had some wine; she had some mineral water—'I never drink alcohol before sunset.'

We went shopping and each bought a Panama hat for the sun; they turned to be made mostly of paper in Amsterdam, rather of straw from Panama, but they were extremely light and comfortable. I bought a Basque linen tablecloth which I thought would go well in the boat.

Eleanor was good company with a sharp wit. She was from Montreal and had been married three times. She was very chatty in the car on the way back to San Sebastien.

'I got married young and had two kids but he was a bastard so I divorced him and married his boss's boss. That was OK for a few years until I found he was cheating on me so my lawyer took him to the cleaners. My third husband, Harvey, was a film producer but he died suddenly of a heart attack whilst filming in South America. I was his only beneficiary. My children have strong careers; my son is a doctor and my daughter is a very successful lawyer. They are self-sufficient so I spend my time at home or travelling. My friend will be better tomorrow so we're off to Santiago de Compostella. She's a devout Catholic and wants to see St James's remains in the cathedral.' She laughed.

'I'm not a catholic.'

She turned to me and smiled. 'I think three husbands is enough, don't you?'

I laughed. She was obviously not a person to cross. We had that in common.

'One wife was enough for me.'

'I have a reservation for dinner tonight at a recommended restaurant in San Sebastian that's difficult to get a booking for. I don't want to eat in the hotel neither do I want to eat on my own. Would you join me?'

I was delighted to. We drove back to the hotel and we agreed to meet in the lobby later.

I confess I had a large glass of wine before meeting Eleanor in the hotel lobby.

We walked down to the old harbour through the old town where bars and restaurants were buzzing. People were drinking wine and eating tapas. Some of them had cured hams hanging from the ceiling.

We went to a fish restaurant where we had clams and sole and Eleanor showed she did drink after sunset. I insisted on paying; why, I'm not sure, but Eleanor was happy to accept my offer.

We walked back to the hotel arm in arm laughing in the warm evening. The bars were still full; San Sebastian was alive with the sound of clinking glass and laughter. She linked her arm into mine. She had been a pleasure to be with. I hadn't enjoyed myself so much for years.

After that, it is a little blurred. I think we went to the bar for a nightcap. But after that, I just can't remember. But I awoke next morning to the smell of her perfume and a feeling of peace. I came to earth with Mr Tibbles jumping on the bed and demanding breakfast.

There was a handwritten note on headed notepaper under my door:

'I had a great time last night. Nice to be treated like a person again. Sorry to have missed you but we had to leave very early. St James is calling. I hope you don't mind but I took a liberty at reception. If you are ever in Montreal (and I hope you will be), please give me a ring.' It was signed Eleanor R.

Just as I finished reading it, the phone went. It was the wife of a colleague from university; she had managed to track me down through my old practice. He had been one of the regular bridge players at university and we had kept in touch after graduating. We had both attended the same congresses where I had met his wife. He had a set up a small practice in Kent which had become very successful and stressful. He had had a heart attack at the gym and was lucky to be alive, thanks to a quick thinking personal trainer. Could I cover for him for a few weeks?

Normally, I would decline but I was in a good place and I had nothing better to do. Besides, it was probably time to head home. After the hotel's huge double bed, Possy wasn't very appealing. I thought if I hurried, we would take three days to get to Kent if we left after breakfast. Today was Friday so I should be able to make it by Monday.

Mr Tibbles and I went down to breakfast, we only just made it, but we sat at our usual table on the terrace; the manager came over to enquire how I had gotten on.

'It was a fantastic day out. Thank you for your suggestions.'

'Mrs Rossini said much the same earlier this morning. I'm glad for you both.' He beamed and walked away.

When I went to pay my bill, I found it had already been settled by Eleanor. So that was what she meant in her note. Well, I would have to buy her diner in Montreal.

I retrieved Possy, loaded her up and we set off northwards.

We got to the practice late on Sunday night and parked in the car park. Next morning I found somewhere more permanent for Mr Tibbles and me, somewhere to park Possy and started work.

It was all very routine and I quickly got into the swing of it. The late spring evenings were long and it was nice to have a pint at a pub after work. Like most vets I was keen to spot the unusual or difficult case. It didn't take long. A young puppy was brought into the clinic in an appalling state. It was a black and white cocker spaniel cross.

The owner said that it had been vaccinated but the certificate didn't look right. When pressed, the owners admitted they had bought it from a carpark near Maidstone for £500 cash after seeing an advert in the local paper.

I admitted the puppy and put it on fluids. I did my best but I knew from past experience that it was hopeless, and it died. It didn't have a chance. Unvaccinated and probably taken from its mother too young then sold at a carpark. I really hated so-called puppy farms.

Two days later, I saw another cocker spaniel cross puppy that was brought in. It was in the same condition, purchased in the same way. It too died. I phoned other vets in the area and they had had the same experience. There must have been eight puppies in the litter.

The seller was always the same; a middle-aged woman with a Welsh accent. She had long grey hair and drove an old, dark blue Volvo Estate.

I couldn't let this go. I put up a big notice in the waiting room warning potential buyers, and scoured the local papers. It wasn't long before I saw the advertisement:

'Eight-week-old Springer Spaniel puppies for sale. Vaccinated and vet-checked. £500.' There was a phone number at the end.

I phoned the number and arranged to meet the woman the next day in a carpark outside Maidstone in the late afternoon. I was careful to park Possy a little way off and walked over to the Volvo.

She opened the boot and there was a cardboard box covered with a soiled blanket. I could see eight brown and white puppies cowering together, trying to find warmth and comfort. They looked thin and their eyes were matted. They were probably six weeks, if that.

'How old are they and how much are they for?' I asked.

'They're eight weeks today. They've been wormed and defleaed. They've had their first vaccine and they're £500 cash.' She sounded well-rehearsed.

I picked one up. It was pitifully thin and tried to suckle on my finger. There was a discharge around its nose and eyes.

'Can I see the parents?' I asked.

'They are off at a show with my husband,' came a practiced response.

'Have you got the vaccine certificate?' I asked, struggling to control my anger.

She showed me a certificate. There was a vaccine sticker and a date and an illegible signature. But no details of the puppy or owner. It was worthless.

'I'll fill in your details when you buy the puppy,' she said, snatching the certificate back.

I handed the puppy back, made my excuses saying I need to speak to my wife, and went back to the car and waited for her to leave. She had a couple of phone calls, then got in her car and left. I followed her. She went down the A20 and turned off towards Bearsted. We went down a country lane to a small row of cottages and she turned into the end one. I drove past, there weren't any other cars, turned Possy around and pulled up into a convenient gateway. It was getting dark and I didn't expect to be here very long. I turned around, Mr Tibbles was asleep. I pulled up the Gladstone bag and rummaged around. I had already decided I was going to dispose of the body at sea.

She could join Mad Dog. So, it didn't matter what drugs I used. I loaded a syringe with large animal immobilon and went up to the house. There was a narrow path along the side of the house. On the other side was a tall hedge. It led to a side door into the kitchen and a shed beyond. She was in the kitchen making herself a cup of tea. I could see the box of puppies on the floor in the utility room behind a child gate. They were eating some cheap tinned dog food.

The back door wasn't locked and whilst the woman was picking up the food bowls, I went in and jabbed her in her bottom. She startled with surprise then turned to face me. She recognised me and picked up a saucepan but the drug started working and she crumpled to the floor, shuddering.

I scooped up the puppies and hurried with them back to Possy. I put them in the shower room then returned for the woman but I could see some headlights in the distance. I just knew that the lights were heading for the woman's house. I ran back to the kitchen. The woman was still having spasms and was very stiff (note to self: use muscle relaxant as well next time). I looked outside the back door; I could see a wheelbarrow. I dragged the woman into it and wheeled her along the path beside the house.

I instinctively crouched down as the car turned into the drive. I stayed motionless as the car was turned off and the driver went into the front door. I pushed the wheelbarrow as fast as I could to Possy, opened the passenger door and hauled the woman into the passenger seat. She was still convulsing but I managed to secure her with the seatbelt. I turned around, picked up the tablecloth I had bought in San Sebastien and draped it over her head. I picked up my paper sun hat and put it on then reached into the glovebox and put on the night driving glasses. I started the van and drove off without turning on the lights. In the distance, I could see someone come out of the house but I was too far down the road.

Once I was on the main road, I stopped the car and looked at the woman. She had made a funny noise five minutes ago but now she was dead. I pulled over to a layby and stopped Possy. I removed the tablecloth, folded it and put it back on the table.

The fridge under the bed was full of wine so I stuffed the bottles where I could, then manhandled the body into the fridge. I had to take her trainers off; she had purple socks and the right one had a hole in the heel. I drew the line at removing anything else. There was a puddle of urine on the seat and a trail to the fridge which I wiped with a kitchen towel and stuffed it in the fridge with her.

I drove Possy over the Thames and called into my old practice that was always staffed. The duty nurse was more than happy to take on the puppies and persuaded the duty vet to accept them. There is nothing as cute as a puppy to a veterinary nurse. I told them I had found them abandoned. There would be no problem finding good homes provided they survived.

I drove up to the marina. It was pitch black and too late to take the boat out. The tides were good for first thing in the morning.

I was tired. It had been a long day and it was time for bed. I parked Possy under a tree, fed Mr Tibbles and went to bed.

I could hear a tapping sound. There was no other sound. Then I could hear a blowing sound in the distance. The tapping was constant and persistent. I turned over but it was still there. Then I saw the grey-haired woman. There was black all around her. She was banging on something. It seemed to be her making the noise. Then I felt a gentle rocking. My mind went into overtime. She was trying to get out of the fridge. I leapt out of bed and turned the light on and rushed outside.

The sun was rising and there was a strong breeze. It was a beautiful summer morning, perfect for sailing. I had parked Possy under a tree and a branch was tapping on the roof. I hadn't secured it properly and the motor home was gently rocking in the wind.

Mr Tibbles meowed for his breakfast.

I made some coffee and fed Mr Tibbles then went down to the moorings and got a cart. I managed to load the woman into it and covered her with the linen tablecloth. I piled on a couple of cases of wine and a blanket. Then Mr Tibbles and I wheeled the cart through the marina entrance and down to the boat. There was no-one about, not even Bob, the harbourmaster.

I unlocked the boat and went up to the anchor winch in the bow with a spare rope from a locker. I had recently invested in a remote control for it so I could operate the anchor from the wheel. With a bit of effort and a lot of swearing, I attached the rope to the winch and took it back to the woman, secured the rope around her and winched her on deck. Once she was secure, I unpacked the rest of the trolley, untied the boat and off we went.

As soon as we were clear of the anchored boats, I put up the sails and we made steady progress to the Maplin Sands. I wrapped the woman's body in some anchor chain then stitched her crudely in a piece of sail. Once at the Whittaker buoy, I found some deeper water and dumped her over the side of the boat.

Mr Tibbles and I anchored for some breakfast then sailed back to the marina.

When I went back to Kent, there was some news about the woman. Speculation was that she had gone off with a Welsh dog breeder in a large white van.

The puppies all did well and found new homes.

After this, I bought some Peugeot white spray paint and sprayed over all the outside letters to give a bit more anonymity.

I never put any food in the fridge under the bed and I never slept in Possy again.

The Flies Strike Back

I could smell the rabbit in the waiting room. It was the sweet fetid smell of fly strike. Common in summer in rabbits that were poorly looked after.

The rabbit was brought in by a mother and her daughter; she was a young dwarf lop female who barely moved when I turned her over. I could see the maggots wriggling to get out of the light. They crawled into her anus and vagina. I can only imagine what that must have felt like. Around the rabbit's tail, the skin and fur was missing and I could see where the maggots had been burrowing into the pink flesh, eating it. The smell was coming from the moist fur.

The rabbit must have been in agony. Her nose hardly twitched and her eyes stared ahead in pain. The rabbit was called Pickles and I admitted her at once and handed her over to one of the nurses called Gemma who would know what to do. In most practices, the veterinary nurses were experts in dealing with this almost entirely preventable disease. As I left the prep room, I could see that Pickles already had an IV catheter in her ear and warmed fluids were flowing through it.

'How long have you had Pickles?' I asked.

'We only got her yesterday. She was a birthday present for my daughter,' the woman replied. The girl was sobbing in the corner of the room.

'Where did you buy her?' I asked.

'Just outside town. There's a small holding that sells pets. The girl who runs it has got all sorts of animals and birds. Will Pickles be alright? Sara will be ever so upset if anything happens to her. She's been begging us for a pet rabbit for ages. We've been to the pet shop and bought a hutch with a run and proper food. We asked them what we needed.'

'Did you check Pickles before you bought her?' I asked.

'My husband bought her. He knows less about animals than I do. We just assumed that the rabbit would be healthy. She was given in a box after he paid cash for her.'

I felt sorry for the woman and her daughter. When I finished surgery, I checked on Pickles. She was sitting snugly in her cage. She had been given pain relief, antibiotics and all the maggots had been removed. She had even started eating some fresh hay.

The next day, the same thing happened. A young couple brought in a dwarf lop with bad fly strike. He was called Chico and his scrotum was red raw where the maggots were eating into him. It was so bad that we had to castrate him immediately.

The couple had bought Chico from the same place. A girl was selling pets for cash at a small holding just outside town.

I saw two more young rabbits in the same condition from the same place. I needed to do something.

I asked the other vets in the practice if they had seen any similar cases. One had seen some mite-ridden chickens and another had seen a guinea pig with very bad teeth. All from the same small holding.

I was off that weekend so I went to see the small holding for myself.

It was just outside of town. The corner of a field had been fenced off. There was a wooded shed by the gateway and some old calf pens behind it. A small field had been cordoned off for some chickens, with a coop in one corner. Right at the back of the field was a small caravan that had seen better days.

There was some washing hanging on a line beside it and a girl smoking a cigarette. An area by the shed had been allocated as car parking. Right at the end was an old blue Ford Fiesta.

I parked the practice car and walked over to the shed. It was about the size of a double garage. Behind it, next to the calf pens, I could see several plastic bags filled with what looked like dead chickens. In the front was a rough counter with a notice saying 'CASH ONLY.' Behind it were a mishmash of sacks of food and bedding and a couple of empty cages that didn't look like they had been cleaned out for ages. Presumably that's where the baby rabbits had been kept.

The first thing I noticed was the smell. It was the rotten smell of decay and death. It reminded me of the post-mortem shed.

I turned to leave.

'Can I help you?' She must have been in her early twenties. Long straight blonde hair and blue eyes, wearing jeans ripped at the knee and a faded white t-shirt advertising a music band I had never heard of. Tattoos smeared her body and she smelt of cigarettes.

'Do you have any rabbits?' I asked.

'Not at the moment. I did have some but they've all gone. They were really popular and went quickly. I sold the last two yesterday. I should have some in a few weeks. You know what they say. "Breed like rabbits."'

Her laughter was cut short by my face.

'Can I have a look around?' I asked.

'Sorry. I was just closing. Maybe another time?' She edged me towards the door.

The fresh air was a relief and I drove back to the surgery. Possy was in the practice carpark and Mr Tibbles was sitting in the passenger seat watching for my return.

It was his teatime and he watched me as I opened a couple of sachets of Sheba. He sniffed them, making sure that they were the right flavour then tucked in.

I had another week to go in Kent. I didn't really know the area but the practice manager put me in touch with the local RSPCA inspector. She was really helpful and was aware of the girl. Apparently, they sold a lot of poultry. Originally, there had been two of them but they had fallen out and parted company. The one who had left had the animal experience. The farmer who leased the land had already warned the girl to get her act together and improve the hygiene. But it looked like the girl had ignored him.

The girl had no licence from the local council and I expected she would be closed down and the animals rehomed.

I probably would have left it at that but the next day, I saw another two rabbits in a really bad way. Their tail areas were awash with maggots and a lot of flesh had been eaten away. They were both very dehydrated and despite all our efforts, they both died. Gemma was really upset as she had tried very hard to get the rabbits to pull through.

I decided that I would take another look at the small holding that evening when it was dark. It was early June so it would be quite late before I got to the small holding. The inspector had told me that the council and RSPCA were going around first thing tomorrow but I wanted to get there before them.

I took the practice car and went back to the small holding. I parked a little way down the lane, retrieved the Gladstone bag and walked the rest of the way. The hut was in darkness but the surrounding fields were lit by moonlight. There was light and music coming from the caravan.

The main door to the hut was locked. I walked around the hut, past the chicken coop where I could hear the chickens settling down for the night. There was a small door at the back which wasn't locked. Outside the door were more plastic bags filled with dead chickens and a couple of dead rabbits.

Once inside, I closed the door and switched on my torch. There were flies buzzing around the empty cages. The smell was awful. I went outside to look at the calf pens. There were four of them; one had a couple of guinea pigs that looked thin and scurfy with mites, and the other three contained rabbits. From what I could tell, each had a male and a female.

The pens were filthy with a mixture of woodchips and straw at the bottom, coated with faeces and urine. There was no food and little water. The bowls were filthy and the rabbits looked thin and depressed. The doe's abdomens were swollen with pregnancy.

I went back into the shed and hunted around for some food and found a large sack of cheap food and a plastic container half full of water. I fed the rabbits and guinea pigs then went back into the shed. There was a bale of musty hay and one of straw. I grabbed a section of hay and distributed it into the pens. The rabbits and guinea pigs ate greedily.

I suppose I could have just gone home. I knew the council and RSPCA would close the girl down and the animals would be rehomed. But I felt sorrow and anger for those people who had bought the rabbits and for Gemma who had tried so hard to save the last two.

The tides were all wrong and I was working tomorrow so there was absolutely no time to get to the boat. But I kept on seeing those poor fly-blown rabbits in my mind. I had to do something.

There was an empty food bowl by the sack of food. I filled it up with as much faecal material as I could from the empty cages then shut the shed and walked quietly over to the caravan.

We used ketamine a lot in rabbits as a safe anaesthetic and practices rarely kept an accurate account in the dangerous drugs book so I had managed to procure a reasonable amount. I had prefilled a syringe of ketamine, diazepam and Tramadol. That should be enough to knock her out for a few hours.

I peered into the caravan and the girl was sitting on the bed, smoking a joint and listening to music blasting out from a stereo. There was a large glass of red wine on a small table beside her, half full, and a bottle beside it. I put on some gloves and waited.

The girl suddenly got up and made for the door. I just managed to go around the side. She walked a few paces along the hedge, then undid her jeans and squatted down to urinate.

I hurried into the caravan, took a swig of the wine from the girl's wine glass and emptied half the contents of the syringe into the glass and the rest into the bottle before hurrying out.

It seemed that the girl was in no hurry to get back to the caravan; she was smoking her joint, looking up at the moon, and I was able to mould myself into the hedge.

I could taste the wine in my mouth. It was really tart. Ketamine is supposed to taste bitter but that wine would disguise anything.

After ten minutes, the girl stubbed out her joint and went back into the caravan. I crept up to a window. She was back on the bed. She took a swig of wine, looked at it quizzically, smelt the bottle, then finished the glass and poured another.

It took longer for the drugs to work than I had thought and it was well after midnight before the girl slumped down on the bed. I gave her another five minutes before going into the caravan. It stank of stale alcohol and smoke. I laid her limp body out on the bed and went out to retrieve the bowl I had collected from the hut. It stank. I smeared the faeces around her hair. Her nose twitched but she remained asleep.

When I had emptied the bowl, I went back to the hut and retrieved the two dead rabbits in their plastic bag. I took them out and laid them at the bottom of the bed then opened a window and waited. I placed the empty wine glass and bottle in the Gladstone bag.

The flies started arriving. I heard them before I saw them. Initially in ones and twos, awoken from their slumber by the smell of faeces. Blue and green sparkling on black bodies. Then more arrived and the caravan was buzzing as they feasted and laid their eggs. I shut the caravan door and rested a chair against it.

I got back home at 2.00am. Mr Tibbles was asleep on the bed. He started purring softly, his eyes shut as I crashed down beside him.

It was midday before I got a call from the RSPCA inspector to go down to the small holding and inspect the animals. I got there just as an ambulance was leaving, siren blaring down the country lane.

There were six rabbits, two guinea pigs and a variety of poultry, all with some sort of disease thanks to the poor conditions.

The three does were all pregnant and underfed. They had sores on their legs from the soiled bedding; these went to a foster home. The three young bucks I would take back to the surgery to be castrated. One of them was covered in fight wounds and his right ear had been torn. The two guinea pigs were crawling with mites which I treated and sent to another fosterer.

The poultry were in very poor condition and covered in mites. There wasn't much I could do for them; no-one would want to foster them in case they were harbouring something nasty. I let the inspector deal with them.

The RSPCA inspector and the council officer had arrived later than they had planned and had found the girl screaming inside the caravan. They removed the chair and found the inside of the caravan black with flies. They had gotten the girl outside and had tried to clean her up but she had been so hysterical and the flies had laid so many eggs it was impossible to remove all the eggs, which would soon hatch out into maggots. The paramedics managed to calm her down but they needed to take her to hospital for a check-up and they would probably have to shave off all her hair.

Had I overreacted? I don't think so. You shouldn't keep animals, let alone profit from them, if you can't look after them properly. Besides, she was alive and not at the bottom of the Crouch. But I suppose she might have a phobia of flies.

Bonnie and Clyde

On my last day in Kent, I thought I saw the same black RAV4 in the carpark. I couldn't be sure but I was starting to get paranoid. I was undecided whether to continue to do locums for a while rather than go back to my 'home practice'. The RAV4 sighting clinched it. I was offered a job near Bicester in Oxfordshire for three weeks. Nothing too taxing but spectacular countryside. I found lodgings in a village called Bucknall a few miles out of the town. The staff and the clients were pleasant enough and I thought the three weeks would pass quickly.

One Wednesday, morning an RSPCA inspector came into the surgery wanting to see a vet. None of the other vets wanted to so I volunteered. He came into the consulting room with a heavy looking black rubbish bag that was dripping with water.

He put it on the table with a thud then opened it up. Inside was a brick and three kittens; two tortoiseshell females and a tabby male. They were about three weeks old and perfectly formed. Someone had deliberately drowned them.

'What happened?' I asked.

'They were found on a building site. The foreman asked a couple of labourers to take them to a local vet. Instead, they put them in a rubbish bag with a brick and drowned them for fun in the local pond.' The inspector sighed. 'The witness who phoned me doesn't want to have anything more to do with the case. I think he just wanted me to fish them out of the pond. The foreman just shrugged his shoulders.'

The inspector laid out the kittens neatly on the table and put the bag and the brick in the bin.

'I know these two lads. This isn't the first time they've done something nasty and I doubt it will be the last. Could you do a post-mortem to confirm that they drowned and let me have a report?'

I nodded. 'What do they know about the mother?'

'I had a quiet look around the site. They've knocked down an old school and are building flats. I couldn't see or hear anything.'

The inspector left. A quick post-mortem revealed all three kittens had been healthy before they were drowned.

One of the receptionists knew of the lads.

'They are a bad lot,' she said. 'They were usually bunking off school when they were younger. Their uncle gave them a job as labourers to placate his sister. But the police are always around their house.'

Apparently, they would hang around the building site after pay day, smoking dope and drinking beer.

That Friday, when I finished work, I went over to the site. There was a big wooden fence around it. The gates were not locked. It was still light and I could hear some laughing and some rocks being thrown. Straight afterwards, I thought I heard a cat meowing. It was a terrified, painful meow.

I picked up the Gladstone bag and slowly pushed the gates open. There was a small prefab office with an old bath and a cement mixer. In front, there was a half demolished school.

Some of the walls had been knocked down, revealing old wooden desks and a blackboard on the far wall scribbled with obscenities. I hurried over to it and peered around the corner.

They were a scrawny pair with long black hair. One was slouched in a chair smoking a joint and a can of beer on the ground beside him. He had a dirty blue cap perched on his head. Next to him was a chair with a can of beer on it. The other lad was hunting around in the rubble in front of the wall. I pulled out the phial of my mixture from my bag and filled up a syringe. I thought I could see the cat holding a paw up inside the exposed schoolroom, under a desk.

'I saw it a minute ago. It must be here somewhere. I'm sure I hit it.' He turned towards his brother. He had a scar across his forehead and kicked some stones in frustration. 'Come and give me a hand, bro. Let's finish it off.'

He got up reluctantly and went over to his brother. I picked up a stone and threw it as far away from the schoolroom as I could. As soon as the stone hit the ground, the lads looked up.

'It must be over there. Come on.' They leapt over the rubble and disappeared. I crept around the side of the hut and emptied half the syringe in each can of beer. I hurried back to Possy. I found a blanket, some gloves and a box I could use for the cat if I found her, and some tinned tuna I could tempt her with. There were some Metacam drops which might help and I put them in the box.

I heard someone shouting at me and turned.

'Please Mister. Help me. Something has happened to my brother.' It was scar face who looked distraught.

I put down the box and followed him into the yard. His brother had collapsed by the chair and was unconscious.

'Can you do CPR?' I asked.

'What's that?' He looked blank.

'Just press down hard on his chest every five seconds as if he was breathing,' I replied.

He crouched down by his brother and started pushing his chest. I put on the gloves with practised ease, looked around, found a suitable brick and hit him as hard as I could on the back of his head. He collapsed beside his brother. There was a trickle of blood coming from the wound on his head.

I hit him again, went back to the van for the box and started looking for the cat. I thought I could see a pair of eyes staring at me. I opened the tin of tuna, mixed some Metacam in it and put it on the floor at the front of the schoolroom. I could see its nose twitch as it smelt it.

It was holding up its left front leg which was swinging. It was obviously broken. Beside the cat was a small ginger bundle—another kitten.

I crawled towards the cat slowly, talking to it all the time. It just stared at me, its pupils wide with pain and fear.

Many people who deal with animals seem to have a natural affinity for certain species. For me, it was cats and horses. Animals seem to know who to trust. I was frequently being asked to see such and such a cat because it was vicious. I always managed to treat them unscathed.

I took off my gloves, dipped my finger in the tuna and stretched it out in front of me towards the cat. I could see that she wanted it. I kept on talking and she sniffed my finger. It was a gentle voice. There was no fear or malice, just reassurance and trust. After five minutes, she picked up the kitten in its mouth and hopped towards me.

A foot away, she put down the kitten and inched forward to lick my finger. Once she started, she couldn't stop and I pushed the tin towards her so she could feed directly from that.

The Metacam must have started working because she seemed to relax and allowed me to pick them both up and wrap them in the blanket in the box. I took them back to Possy, pushed the toilet out of the way and left them in the shower. I slipped on another pair of gloves.

The drugged brother was still out cold but the one I had hit over the head was moaning and starting to gain consciousness. There was a sledgehammer by the office and I picked it up and hit his arm as hard as I could. I could hear the crack as it broke. There was a gasp and a groan.

'See how you like someone breaking your arm,' I muttered.

The bath by the cement mixer was half full of water. I turned on the hose to fill it then dragged the brother over to it. When it was nearly full, I turned the tap off and thrust his head into the water until the bubbles of air stopped. Then I did the same to the other.

By this time, it was getting dark. I opened the yard gates and reversed Possy in. Then I removed their boots and squashed them head to toe into the fridge. I picked up the two beer cans and emptied the water from the bath. I expected the police to find some blood if they looked but it wouldn't be mine and I always wore surgical gloves.

I drove Possy out, closed the gates and went back to the practice. It wasn't open twenty-four hours but one of the nurses called Jenny lived in a small flat above it.

Jenny was in and reluctantly agreed to help me. Reluctant that is until she saw the kitten, then she went into overdrive. We managed to put a drip on the mother and bandage the affected leg. I injected her with some antibiotics and some more painkiller and left, with Jenny bottle-feeding the kitten.

I drove back to my digs in Bucknall, showered and had a couple of hours' sleep then drove to the marina in Essex with Mr Tibbles, dumping the cans of beer on the way.

The marina was fairly busy when I arrived. Mr Tibbles had smelt where the other cat had been but showed no interest. I took him and the two bodies onto the boat, using the anchor winch and rope, which made it so easy.

It was a pleasant sail. There was a regatta at the marina opposite so I had to wait until it was clear before I attended to the brothers. There was still plenty of spare sail but each body required at least three meters and nearer four meters of anchor chain. If there were many more, I might have to rethink. The two brothers slid into the water easily and quickly sank out of sight. Who would suspect where they were? I am sure the police would think their disappearance was gang-related.

When I got back to shore, I phoned up the practice to see how the cat and kitten were doing. The mother was stable and the kitten bottle feeding well but the senior vet had thrown his toys and wanted to amputate the leg and then try and find a foster home. I managed to placate him saying that I would not only do the operation in my own time but would pay for the necessary repair as well.

That seemed to suffice and Jenny agreed to help me on Sunday night and would start to get everything ready before I returned.

I checked the post at my house; there was nothing of interest. I wrote cheques for the bills and drove back to Bicester after lunch on Sunday. Jenny had everything ready.

We took some x-rays. It was a comminuted fracture of the left humerus. It wouldn't be that easy. It would need screwing and plating, and patience. I just hoped the radial nerve hadn't been affected. But she was a young cat and I would rather try to repair the fracture than just amputate.

Three and a half hours later, after much swearing and cursing, we finished. Jenny was a star as she had to scrub in and hold the bones whilst I fixed the plate on the broken bones. I'm no supervet but the post-operative x-ray looked OK and the kitten was doing well.

Whilst the cat recovered, we cleaned up the operating theatre. Jenny asked what was going to happen to the cats.

'They'll have to be rehomed. I expect they'll go to a foster home until the kitten is weaned then the mum will have to be spayed and a home found,' I said.

I could see Jenny was totally bonded to both animals and a bit disappointed.

'Do you think I could adopt them? I'm only staying here temporarily, I'm moving into my new house in a couple of weeks.'

'I don't see why not.'

Jenny beamed. 'I'm going to call them Bonnie and Clyde.' She smiled, bottle feeding the kitten.

'You'll be calling them Jocasta and Oedipus if you don't get them neutered.'

She looked at me as if I was speaking Greek.

Jasper and the Carrots

That was my last day. I packed up my digs and stopped off to see how the mother cat and kitten were doing. Jenny was fussing over them and both seemed fine. The mother even managed a little purr when she saw me. I saw the senior vet looking at the post-op x-rays.

He looked at me and smiled. 'Better than I could have done. Jenny's going to take them both on so there won't be any charge.' We shook hands and I said my goodbyes.

I was on cloud nine until I left the practice and saw a black RAV4 parked on the other side of the road. There was an overweight middle-aged man sitting in the driver's seat. He was bald with a thin moustache and wore thick spectacles.

I thought about going over to him but thought better of it. I had been asked to go back to my old practice. The senior partner was retiring and had asked if I could cover until a suitable replacement was found. It meant I could live at home and get some sailing in, but I scribbled down the number plate just in case.

The senior partner was embarrassingly happy to see me. He greeted me like a long-lost friend. He and his wife were moving down to Devon and I was invited to his farewell party at a local hotel.

I recognised a lot of old clients and a few ex-assistants who had been invited back. The drink was free-flowing, sponsored by a drug company. I found myself talking to Wendy who had been working at the practice for longer than I had been. She was nursing a large glass of red wine and looked as if she had already had a few.

'How are you getting on?' She slurred. 'I was sorry to hear about your wife.'

'Thanks. I still miss her.'

Wendy looked nonplussed, unsure of saying anything else. Something seemed to be on her mind. 'I have a confession to make.' She gulped the rest of her red wine and put the empty glass down on a table. 'Do you remember your hamster? Hammy, wasn't it?'

I nodded.

'He was poisoned, wasn't he?' Wendy got a refill from a waiter and took a big swig. 'I think I was responsible.'

I looked quizzically at her.

'A client brought in a bag of hamster food. Then a few minutes later, another brought in some coloured seeds they thought were poison and wanted a vet to check. I put these seeds next to the hamster food and I think you must have taken them with the bag because when I went to look for them, they were both gone. I meant to tell you when it happened but you were so distraught, I didn't have the heart.'

She looked terrible.

'Don't worry, Wendy. I forgive you.' I put my hand on her shoulder. 'It was a long time ago and a lot has happened since them.'

She looked relieved and embarrassed and went off to the ladies' room.

I suppose that I should have been upset. But Wendy had always been very kind to me, unlike my sister. No doubt, sooner or later, I would have done something.

I started work the next day. The senior partner had given up operating a long time ago and just consulted in the morning and evening with the occasional visit. I was allocated his hours and given his old practice vehicle as Possy definitely wasn't suitable.

The practice was busy and the younger assistants always grateful for my advice; whether they took it was up to them.

I enjoyed the house visits; seeing inside people's houses was fascinating. I also was asked to see the occasional horse.

Several of my old clients brought their pets to see me and told their friends, so fairly quickly, my consulting slots filled up. After morning surgery, I would have a cup of coffee then do any visits that had been booked in. It gave me a chance to see the different areas I hadn't been to before.

One visit was to do a stitch-up on a horse near Paglesham. Nearby was a well-known pub where I could have a late lunch.

The house was a large red brick building that had once belonged to someone in the oyster trade, or so the owner told me. There was a large garden with a well-stocked kitchen garden and a paddock with a basic stable in it. Next to it was a small field with an old Morris Traveller parked in the gateway with a straw bale sticking out of the back. The field was an absolute mess. It hadn't been poo-picked for a long time and there were old car tyres and rusting farm machinery scattered in the un-mowed grass. There was a ramshackle stable in one corner.

The owner's retired horse had cut itself on some barbed wire the owner hadn't known about but had probably come from next door. The stitch-up was easy and just as I was finishing, I heard a pony whinny. It was a sad cry of a pony in pain.

'It belongs to Maggie. She rents the paddock off the farmer. Has done for years but she doesn't come up here much anymore.' The woman sighed. 'There is precious little grass. I toss over some hay now and again. But there's never any gratitude. I think the pony has probably had it.'

I put in the last stitch and wandered over. It was a skewbald pony that was peering over the fence. Its feet were too long, coat matted and un-brushed and it looked thin and hungry. A plump woman with unkempt grey hair was filling up an old bath.

'Hello Maggie,' my client said politely over the fence. 'This is the vet.'

'Morning Gill,' Maggie replied tersely. 'Don't need one of them. I can sort out all Jasper's problems myself. There's nothing a dose of Epsom salts or some apple cider vinegar won't cure.' Maggie turned away, took the straw bale out of the car and tossed it into a lean-to by the stable.

'Can't stay here talking all day. Got things to do.' Maggie got into her car and drove off.

'Could I give Jasper a carrot from your garden? I noticed that you were growing some.'

The woman smiled and nodded. 'Take two or three. I've more than we can eat. I'm sorry about Maggie. She's an only child who never married. Her parents had a successful furniture business and had a big house in Southchurch where

Maggie still lives.' The woman laughed. 'She has plenty of money but you wouldn't think it the way she dresses.'

I pulled up three carrots, dusted off the mud and fed them to Jasper. He ate them, stalks and all.

'Thank you,' I said. 'I'll come back in just over a week to remove the sutures.'

I found my way to the pub, ordered a pie and chips and sat outside in the garden, nursing a pint of beer. It should be out of my system before evening surgery.

A week later, I went to remove the sutures and took some carrots with me. The wound had healed well but Jasper was in an even worse state. He gave a little whinny when he saw me but he could barely walk over to the fence so I threw the carrots on the ground as close as I could to him.

'That doesn't look very good,' I remarked. 'Really needs to see a vet.'

'Maggie doesn't believe in vets. You heard what she said. She believes in home remedies; apple cider vinegar, Epsom salts, that sort of thing.'

I looked back at the pony. It really wasn't very well.

'Let me know if it gets any worse. I hate seeing an animal suffer because of its owner.'

I drove home, regretting that I should have done more.

The next day, I got a call that Jasper was down. By the time I got to the field, he was on his side, breathing badly and bicycling with his legs. Around him was flattened grass. Every now and then, he would grunt in pain. His stomach was swollen.

'How long has he been like this for?' I asked the woman who had called me.

'I'm not sure; he was like this when I went to feed the horses their breakfast,' she replied anxiously.

'Have you tried the owner?' I asked.

'Maggie's not answering her phone.'

I couldn't leave Jasper like this but I needed a second opinion from another vet before I did anything drastic.

'I'll give him a pain-killing injection and try and get a second opinion. Can I use your phone?' The woman nodded and we went into the house.

I managed to get hold of one of the other vets who knew a little about horses and we both agreed if the situation was hopeless, I should put Jasper down even if we couldn't get hold of the owner. Jasper was definitely suffering.

He was no better after the injection. If anything, he was worse.

'I don't think that I can do anything. Have you tried the owner again?'

The woman nodded then shook her head. 'No reply.'

'I don't think that I have any option. Jasper is in a lot of pain. I think I should put him to sleep.'

The woman nodded in assent.

I got an injection out of the car and gave it to Jasper. His breathing shallowed and slowed, he gave two large gasps and then he was gone.

'Thanks for coming out and doing that. I couldn't just leave him.' The woman sounded grateful.

I put everything back in the van and headed off to the pub for a well-earned drink. I had just settled down to a beer when Maggie stormed in.

'Murderer!' She shrieked. 'You've killed my Jasper. Murderer!'

All conversation in the pub ceased and everyone looked from Maggie to me.

I felt the blood drain from my face.

'Your pony was in agony. I had no option.' I tried to placate her in a soft, even voice.

'You poisoned him with those carrots you gave him!' She shouted. Then she pointed at me. 'Murderer!'

I could see the waitress trying to bring my pie. I shrugged my shoulders.

'Can we talk about this outside?'

'There's nothing to talk about; you've just killed my horse. I'm going to the police.' She stormed out.

I looked at the pie that had been delivered. It didn't look that appetising. I mumbled my apologies to the waitress and left. I turned back as I reached the door and saw the pub's customers looking at me as if I was some kind of mass murderer.

The next day, Maggie made a formal complaint to the practice, the police and the local RSPCA. The latter two weren't interested but the practice was worried about the effect on the business. It was made worse when Maggie started coming to the practice when I was consulting and sitting in the waiting room with a home-made placard declaring that I had murdered Jasper.

The post-mortem on Jasper showed that he had very little body fat one and ring bone in both his front legs. He had had a twisted small intestine and there was nothing other than major surgery that anyone could have done. He wasn't insured and it was doubtful he could have been taken somewhere in time. Inside his small intestine were pieces of carrot as well as small bits of rubber and metal.

Maggie knew my consulting hours and would be in the surgery when I arrived, silent and determined with her placard. I dreaded every day. For the first time in my professional career, I didn't want to go to work. The receptionists did what they could but short of frog-marching her out of the surgery, there was little they could do. A general unease hung around the clinic when I was there and the requests from clients to see me dried up.

She informed the practice manager she had made a formal complaint to the Royal College of Veterinary Surgeons. I was summoned to the practice manager's office and was asked to write a full account. I was then suspended from working on full pay until the Royal College had finished their investigations.

I didn't need the money but I was angry that an act of innocent animal kindness had resulted in my being shunned by the practice and my ex-clients.

I knew from other vets' experiences that the Royal College would be pedantic and drawn out. The last thing I wanted was for the Royal College to start looking into my affairs. I wanted to stay below their radar. I phoned the company that provided professional indemnity who were politely unhelpful and told me to wait for the complaint to arrive to see exactly what was being alleged. That was not my way.

My suspension gave me an opportunity to create a new concoction and I went back to digitalis, diazepam and phenobarbitone. This time, I added more digitalis to stop the heart. I managed to create a clear liquid but it tasted a little bitter. However, if I mixed it with strong tea, I couldn't taste it at all, even without sugar. I made up 100mls and put it in an empty water bottle in the fridge.

Then I had an idea. I retrieved a box of sugar cubes from the back of the coffee and tea cupboard. I never used them but to my surprise, they were still in date. I made up another 20mls of the solution as concentrated as I could, which I put in a syringe. It tasted really bitter. I took four sugar cubes and put them on a small plate with some kitchen roll underneath on the window sill which caught the afternoon sun. Then I carefully put four drops on each cube. I repeated this every day until all of the solution was used up. Two of the cubes survived and I placed them carefully on top the other cubes.

I started driving around Southchurch to see if I could spot the Morris Traveller; there couldn't be many left on the road. It took a while because she had parked it in a rickety black wooden garage behind her house. I happened to see her driving it one evening with a queue of cars concertinaed behind her. She slowly swung it into a side road and into a garage with practiced ease.

The next day, I went around to the house. It was a large detached red brick double-fronted affair. In its time, it must have been very impressive but now, there were faded black wooden beams separating, peeling white render and rotten wooden sash windows barely holding in the glass panes. The garden was overgrown and the two rusty gates at the front didn't look as if they had been opened for years. It was a house neglected and unloved.

I wasn't sure what I was going to do. I couldn't confront her face to face. She wasn't the type of person you could reason with. I just wanted the Royal College proceedings to stop and my life back to normal. There was a wooden gate leading from the back garden to the garage. The car wasn't in the garage so I decided to explore further. The back gate wasn't locked so I pushed it open.

The dustbin was buzzing with flies and was full of half-eaten cans and ready meal packets and empty milk cartons. The garden was unkempt. Rusty garden machinery peered out of overgrown grass. A fox looked up and casually exited through a hole in the fence. Panicking birds called frantically from dense shrubs and bushes. There was an outside toilet next to a coal store and then a black door leading into the house. It wasn't locked so I went in.

The kitchen was hot and dark and it smelt musty and unaired. The black and white tiled floor was covered with bags and boxes. These were haphazardly scattered around a huge oak table covered with cutlery and crockery except at one end where there was a placemat with a pile of magazines beside it and a huge armchair laden with flattened cushions.

In the middle of the table was a flower vase with a couple of fresh roses. On one side was a large Aga throwing out heat. Above it, pots and pans hung randomly. Next to it, there was a butler sink full of dirty plates. In a corner was a large faded yellow fridge. Inside the fridge was some dried mouldy cheese, a box of eggs, a shelf packed with oven-ready meals and two cartons of milk that were in date. Next to the fridge was a wooden door with a window of dirty fine wire mesh opening into a larder packed with packets and tins, many long past their expiry date.

On the floor was a wine box with half a dozen bottles of sherry. But there were two packets of tea that were within date and obviously used.

I went through a door into the rest of the house; each room was packed with dark furniture stuffed with boxes and bags laden with old books and papers, knickknacks and photograph albums. It was a hoarder's den.

The only things that seemed recent purchases were the tins, oven-ready meals, tea and milk. That seemed to be what Maggie lived off.

I retraced my steps and drove home to think. No-one would miss her and the Royal College would pursue me no further and I could get back to work. I needed to dope the milk to sedate her enough for me to fill her up with morphine and get her onto the boat. The two cartons had been identical and were the same as the empty ones in the bin. I could buy one, replace some of the milk with some of the new solution or I could just use the large animal immobilon. I decided on the latter as it would be more potent. But after the last time I used immobilon, I would add some diazepam as a relaxant. I just needed to work out Maggie's routine.

I wasn't working so it wasn't that difficult. Possy would have been too obvious and I didn't have the use of a practice car so I bought a bicycle. I found a bench near the house where I could read and watch.

Maggie rarely went out as she no longer had Jasper to visit. What she did in the house I had no idea but she just went once a week to the shops but not on any particular day; on Sundays, she went to the local church for the 11.00am service when she was gone for about an hour. That would be when to swap the milk.

High tide was about eight o'clock that Sunday evening. Not perfect but doable.

I bought the milk from the local supermarket, syringed out 5mls and replaced it with a diazepam immobilon mixture. I put a tiny blob of candle wax on the carton where I had syringed out the milk.

I decided I would cycle to Maggie's house, make sure that she went to church, swap the milk then go back home. The practice let me borrow a van for an afternoon. It would be much less conspicuous than Possy.

It all went surprisingly easily. I removed the milk from the fridge and left the doctored carton, and then sat on the bench with my book. She came back from church just after midday and I waited on the bench. After an hour, I went up to the house. When I opened the door to the kitchen, she was slumped in the chair. There was a half-drunk mug of tea on the table which I emptied down the outside toilet. I found an old rug rolled up on the floor of one of the bedrooms. I wrapped her in it and left her in the kitchen and cycled home.

I returned in the van. There were about three hours before high tide. I reversed the van so it was as close as possible to the back door. There were no lights on and there didn't seem to be anyone about. I managed to drag and push her into the back of the van. I got to the end of the street when I remembered the milk.

I turned the van around and drove back to the house. I rushed into the house and retrieved the milk from the fridge and replaced it with the carton I had removed earlier. I thought I heard something in one of the bedrooms but I was in too much of a hurry to care. What I didn't see was a black RAV4 parked a little way down the street.

By the time I got to Possy, Maggie was stiff and dead. I put the milk in the fridge instinctively and got the boat keys, a cool box with some food and drink and Mr Tibbles. She seemed heavier and more difficult to move when I loaded her into Possy. We drove off to the marina, Mr Tibbles sitting on the seat next to me.

It was getting dark when we got to the marina and most of the pleasure sailors had left the marina and there were just a few lights in the houseboats.

I loaded Maggie and the carpet onto a trolley and wheeled it to the boat with the cool box perched on top and Mr Tibbles running alongside. We dumped the body past the Whittaker buoy and took our time to return to the marina, enjoying a cup of tea in the late evening air. Everything was dark with the stays clinking in a gentle breeze. It was time to go home.

When I got home, there was a message on the answering phone from the policeman who had been at the dog-fight.

'I owe you a favour so I thought you should know. We had a private detective at the station earlier today asking questions about you. He said something about you using a horse drug on people. He had to go to Belfast tomorrow so he was going to come around to see you later on this evening to ask a few questions.'

As soon as the message finished, there was a knock at the front door.

Narcan

He was a middle-aged man. Plump and bald with a thin ginger moustache and piercing blue eyes staring through black spectacles. Behind him, parked on the other side of the road, was a black RAV4.

He smiled as he put his foot in the doorway.

'I'm Jackson Jennings of JJ's investigation agency. I'm a private investigator working for Mrs Betty Morris. Can I come in? I won't be a minute. I just have a few questions for you.' He spoke quietly and quickly and was in the hallway before I had a chance to think.

I led him through to the kitchen. Mr Tibbles took one look at him, hissed and went upstairs.

He took off his coat, put it on the back of a chair and sat down at the kitchen table. He pulled out a notebook from a bag. 'I apologise it's so late but I have to go to a conference in Belfast tomorrow and I didn't feel this could wait any longer.' He looked at his notes. 'Do you recall Robert Morris?' He looked at me accusingly, his eyes fixed on mine.

Of course, I didn't. I had no idea who he was talking about. The detective looked a little disappointed.

'He was castrated by someone who had surgical experience last year. His life has been irreparably ruined. The police weren't that interested in investigating the case. Robert was known to them as a lazy lout who was always getting into trouble. But he is the apple of his mother's eye and she is determined to find out who did it.'

The detective paused, rummaged around in his bag and pulled out a small clear plastic bag. It contained a sterilisation indicator strip.

'I found this near where Robert was castrated.' The detective put it back in his bag. 'Do you recognise it?' He looked accusingly at me.

'I've seen many in operating kits that I've opened but that particular one. No.' *That was careless of me*, I thought. But I hadn't touched it so there was nothing linking it to me.

'Do you remember Sharon Fitzroy and Craig Rogers?' The detective asked.

I shook my head. Again, I had no idea who they were.

'They were petty drug dealers who died in a house fire a few months ago. He drove a BMW. I'm told that they bought their dog, a collie cross, to see you the day before the fire. Apparently, they took it home with them. But you operated on an identical one you claimed was a stray on the day after the fire.'

'I don't remember all the animals I have operated on.' But I did remember Bella and seeing the black RAV4 parked in the street.

'I've been following your career with interest. Your sister, mother, grandmother and wife have all died. Nothing suspicious has been reported. Terribly bad karma.' The detective looked at me but I said nothing. 'The places you work all seem to coincide with missing persons.' The detective shuffled through his papers.

'I've been trying to trace all the practices where you have worked. Essex. Kent. Oxfordshire. I have all the dates somewhere.' He produced a notebook with cuttings from local newspapers. The word "missing" was prominent in all the headlines.

I had had enough. It was time to act. 'I am just making a cup of tea; would you like some?'

The detective nodded. 'Thank you. I am a bit parched.'

'I'm just going to the bathroom,' I said quietly. The detective didn't seem to hear.

I went into my office and retrieved a syringe of Narcan from the Gladstone bag, flushed the downstairs toilet and hurried back. The detective hadn't moved.

The kettle eventually boiled and I put a separate teabag into two mugs.

'Do you take milk?' I asked, opening the fridge. The only milk was the milk from Maggie's house.

The detective looked up from his notebook, stared at the milk carton and smiled. 'Yes please, and two sugars.'

I poured the water into mugs, stirred with a teaspoon and added milk to both and the two doctored sugar lumps into his. They just made it into the mug before they disintegrated. The detective watched me then went back to his notebook. I took the mugs over to the table and sat down.

As I took a small sip from mine, I put my hand in my pocket, took out the syringe of Narcan, flicked off the syringe cap and jabbed it into my thigh, trying to remain as expressionless as I could.

The detective seemed to make the same movement.

'Let me tell you what I think.' He stirred his tea and took a large swallow. 'I needed that. I think in your job, you sometime see cases of animal cruelty that you passionately want to do something about. Euthanasia is something you do every day. It's become part of your routine. It's what you vets do if you can't fix an animal. You have access to many drugs, especially opiates, and you use them for your revenge.'

'I asked at the vets what drugs could be lethal to humans. I was told pentobarbitone would be impossible to disguise by mouth because of its colour and taste. Morphine would work but you would need quite a high dose and then they mentioned a drug used in horses and large wild animals. Immobilon.' He looked at the tea in his mug.

'You see yourself as a sort of veterinary vigilante for animals that have been mistreated. A "Vetilante".' He took another gulp of tea and stared straight at me.

'In reality, you are nothing more than a psychopath who is so used to putting people's pets to sleep, you've blurred the boundary between humans and animals. You are using people's actions with their pets as an excuse. What you really enjoy is killing people with drugs.'

He turned the empty teacup over in his hand. 'But I didn't have any real evidence. Not until now. Would you mind bringing over the milk carton you used in the tea?'

I went over to the fridge and brought the opened carton over to him.

'I think that you poisoned Maggie James with this milk. My bet is that it contains this horse drug they told me about. I went to her house to retrieve it but you just beat me to it. I had to hide in a bedroom when you came back. I thought you were bound to see me. Now, you've given some of the milk to me. But I took precautions.' He placed an empty syringe on the kitchen table and drained his mug of tea.

'I've drunk all the tea so there should be plenty of the drug in my bloodstream. This milk carton with your fingerprints on, the drug in it and in my body should be enough to put you away for a very long time. I spoke to the local police earlier today. They are expecting my call. I just need to give them this milk carton and get someone to take a blood sample from me, and that will be that.' The detective looked very pleased with himself.

I picked the syringe up; it was labelled "Narcan".

'Useful drug, that.' I took my own syringe out of my pocket and laid it beside his.

'Painful intramuscular injection, isn't it?' I said, rubbing my thigh. 'It is a great antidote for opiate poisoning like the etorphine in immobilon which, you are right, is in the milk. But immobilon also contains a sedative, acepromazine, and naloxone is useless against that. There was also some diazepam in the milk and there were other drugs in the sugar cubes. Narcan doesn't work against those either.'

The detective's face dropped.

'Digitalis,' I continued. 'Diazepam and phenobarbitone. Digitalis slows the heart, diazepam is a sedative which potentiates the effects of digitalis, and phenobarbitone potentiates the acepromazine sedative effects. I don't think that you have long before you start to feel sleepy. In fact, it looks like the drugs are already starting to work.'

The detective looked at me with fear in his eyes. He stood up and tried to get the milk carton but he missed and it fell on the floor. He slipped on the spilt milk and landed heavily on the tiles. I slowly walked over to the sofa and grabbed a cushion. I stared down at him. He was trying to remain conscious but the drugs were taking hold.

'Goodbye, Mr Detective,' I whispered to him.

I held the cushion over his face and pressed hard until he went limp.

Mr Tibbles appeared in the doorway, looked at me, meowed and went into the kitchen in search of food. I gave him a sachet five minutes later.

I loaded the detective into Possy and Mr Tibbles and I set off for the marina.

Airport

The kitchen was as I had left it. I poured the rest of my tea down the sink, cleared up the split milk and put the dirty mugs into some hot water in the sink. I washed them thoroughly then put them back on the shelf.

I had put the detective's case and papers with his body so they would all be now at the bottom of the Crouch.

I parked Possy on the concrete hard stand I had made at the side of the house in front of the garage. She was too tall to fit inside it. I thoroughly steam cleaned the inside from top to bottom then, exhausted, went to bed.

First thing in the morning, I phoned up one of the nurses who I knew would be happy to look after Mr Tibbles whilst I was away. I dropped him off at the practice with his bed and some of his favourite food. He wasn't impressed and howled at me. I knew as soon as I was gone, the nurses would spoil him.

I phoned up the marina and arranged for the boat to be taken out of the water, deep cleaned and two coats of anti-foul applied. They would also service the engine, repair any dents or cracks and then wax and polish it. It would be like new.

I packed my bags, checked the house for the fifth time and set off in the detective's RAV4 for Heathrow Airport, his coat on the passenger seat. I left the Gladstone bag in a left luggage locker at a railway station on the way.

I parked the RAV4 in the long-term carpark of Heathrow Terminal 5, put on the detective's coat and took the courtesy bus to the terminal, trying to keep well away from other travellers. Inside the terminal, I went to the toilets and threw the car keys and coat into a rubbish bin. I checked in with BA, took the fast track through security and made my way to the business-class lounge.

Here I was on my third glass of champagne and enjoying some sandwiches and cake before my flight. The PIC or preliminary investigation committee of the Royal College would draw a blank. I had sent them a letter asking for more details from Jasper's owner. I knew that there would be no more correspondence from the complainant and the case would be shelved and forgotten about. I would be able to continue practicing with a clear record.

I was not sure what I was expecting from Canada or from Eleanor, but I needed the break.

I expect I'll be back in the UK, keeping an eye out for those people who abuse animals. I suppose the detective was right; I do get a buzz from killing people who abuse their pets. So, let this be a warning to you. Be careful how you treat your animals. Be kind, or you might have to answer to the Vetilante!

www.ingramcontent.com/pod-product-compliance
Lightning Source LLC
Chambersburg PA
CBHW061526050726
47593CB00002B/687